RAIN HAMMERS THE METAL ROOF.

A blue-white flash of lightning illuminates Klink and Klank, sitting side by side in the driest spot of the old barn—the horse stalls.

Klank stretches out a beat-up ax-handle leg.

Klink flexes his squeaky barn-door-hinge elbow, closes his webcam eye.

Freight-train-loud wind roars through the cracks in the barn walls.

A *SMAAAAASH CRAAAACK!* peal of thunder rocks the whole world.

Klank butt-jumps sideways, closer to Klink.

"Klink," says Klank.

Klink opens his eye. "What?"

"Are you ever afraid?"

Klink pretends to think about this for three seconds, because he knows this makes Klank feel better. "No. Because we are robots. We are never afraid. Or mad. Or sad."

Klank nods his dented vegetable-strainer head. **"Yeah. That is what I thought."**

The storm wind blasts open the hayloft shutter with a mad *BAAAAAM!*

"YIIIIKES!" Klank wraps Klink in both his irrigation-hose arms.

Klink hands Klank his stuffed teddy bear.

Klank unwraps his arms, strokes the soft fur, and rocks back and forth.

"Now power down, and stop worrying," says Klink.

"OK," says Klank. He pats his teddy bear, rocking it in his arms.

The storm howls and rages and shakes the whole barn. Lightning flashes. Thunder crashes.

Klank tries to power down and stop worrying.

But he can't stop the thinking and the feeling . . . that this is the end of the world.

...ANK ...TEIN

and the BIO-ACTION GIZMO

JON SCIESZKA

ILLUSTRATED BY BRIAN BIGGS

AMULET BOOKS

NEW YORK

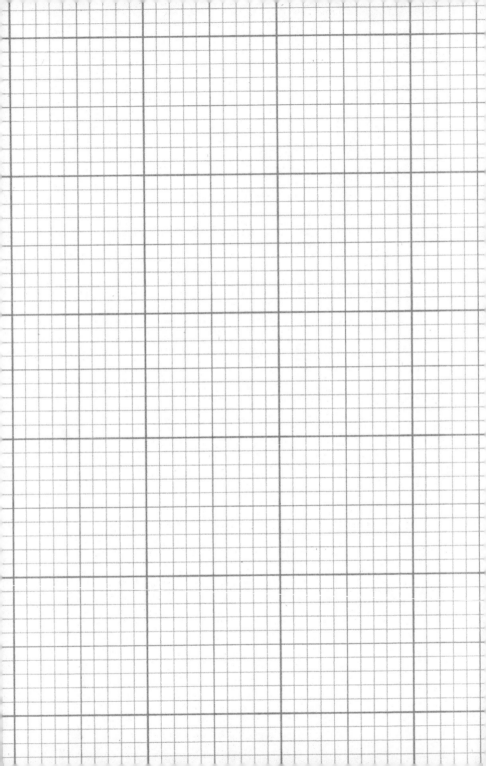

THE BLUE PLASTIC BAG WITH AN EARTH/HEART LOGO FLIES OUT THE back window of an oversized blue truck.

It hits the asphalt road and rolls in the wake of the speeding truck like a futuristic manmade tumbleweed.

The truck makes a sharp right turn.

The plastic tumblebag rolls straight on.

It tumbles

down a ditch

over clumps of waving amber grasses

past an oak tree swaying in the breeze

and under a carved wooden sign reading

MIDVILLE FOREST PRESERVE.

A gust of wind blows the indestructible bag straight up, spooking a mother deer and her fawn.

The bag chases after the deer across the sunny meadow. It spins off down a hill toward three figures standing at the edge of the woods.

The biggest figure spreads his aluminum flex-duct arms wide and booms, **"AHHHHHHH NATURE!"**

The smallest figure rolls his single webcam eye. "**You may not have noticed—but you are the most unnatural thing out here.**"

Klank, because of course it is robot Klank, ignores Klink and spins around in a happy circle.

"Who doesn't love birds and bees and flowers and trees?"

Frank Einstein, kid genius, bends down to inspect the stump of the freshly cut tree.

"It looks like someone doesn't. Who would be cutting down trees inside the Midville preserve?"

The guys hear the sound of machinery in the distance.

The blue plastic bag flies up and twirls in a mini-twister above Klink, Klank, and Frank.

Klank spins and stumbles against Klink.

"Hey! Watch it!"

"Watch what? Ha ha ha," laughs Klank. He spreads his robot arms again and sucks a huge breath of fresh forest air into his ventilation port.

He also, unfortunately, sucks the plastic bag into his ventilation port.

FFFFFFFFFFT! The bag plugs Klank's port. It cuts off the air cooling his heat-producing brain circuits.

SSSSSSHSHHHHHHHHHHH! The plastic bag catches in Klank's mechanical movement wheels. The plastic shreds. Small threads wind around every cog and wheel.

Klank staggers.

Klink props him up.

BLLLLLLLLLLLUUUUUUUGGGGHHHHHH! The

plastic shreds melt. And drip into every crack and corner of Klank's processor.

Klank's music slows.

Klank's left eye blinks EMERGENCY red.

Klank's arms and legs start to twitch.

Klank stops spinning and shorts out.

"Alert," beeps Klink. "Klank may lose balance. His trajectory may intersect with this tree. This collision may bring it down."

"I think he'll be okay," says Frank.

The blue-plastic-bag drips gum up Klank's gyroscope. Which controls Klank's balance.

Klank's heavy-duty-trash-can body leans, and tips. Klink can't hold him.

"Uh-oh," says Frank.

"Unfortunately," beeps Klink. "I am always right."

Klank falls heavily into the giant tree. The trunk snaps . . . and the entire tree falls with a thunderous *CRASSSSSH!*

Smashing Klank into a pile of broken parts in the middle of the forest.

≋ ‖ ⦸

2

SCREWDRIVER!" CALLS FRANK EINSTEIN.

"Screwdriver," answers Watson, slapping the tool into Frank's outstretched hand.

Frank unscrews the metal plate covering Klank's gyroscope.

"Wire cutters!"

Watson reaches into his expanding rope bag, hands the tool to Frank. "Wire cutters."

Frank snips the wire on Klank's leg motor.

"Power drill!"

Watson digs through his bag. "Hammer, wrench, clamps, saw . . . no drill."

Frank looks up from the pile of disconnected Klank parts.

"What? How am I supposed to fix Klank with no drill?!"

"I threw everything into my EMERGENCY bag and came as fast as I could," says Watson. "Maybe you can use the screwdriver."

"You should have brought a bigger bag—with more tools!"

"This is the best bag. I use it all the time."

Frank frowns. "Sorry, Watson." Frank realizes he is more mad at himself for not being able to fix Klank than he is mad at Watson and his bag.

"You may use my drill," says Klink. "Part of my farm-trip tool additions."

"Nice work, Klink," says Frank. He guides Klink's drill to Klank's bent main-drive gear.
Frank pulls it out and hands
it to Klink. "I think all we
have to do is straighten
this, rewire the drive motor,
and knock out some body
dents."

Klink examines
the gear with his
single-eye cam.

"No. This can not be fixed."

"Of course it can," argues Frank. "Everything can be fixed."

Klink reexamines the gear.

Klank, in pieces, does not move.

"*BRARRRRRRRRRR!*" screams a chain saw deeper in the forest.

"*RRRRUUUUUHHHHHRRRRR!*" buzzes the deep hum of a drill from over the hill.

"No. Your statement is not true. Not everything can be fixed."

3

leans out of the cab of the **EARTH/HEART** logging truck, yelling through a bullhorn.

"Faster, faster, faster!"

"*BRRARRRRRRRRRRRRR,*" howls a dozen chain saws.

CRASSSSHHHHH! A big oak tree drops.

One of the loggers stops to take a drink of water. "What's the big rush?"

"I don't know. But the Big Boss says we have one more week to cut as much as we can."

"That's crazy."

"Faster, faster, faster!"

The other logger shrugs. He starts up his chain saw.

And takes on another oak.

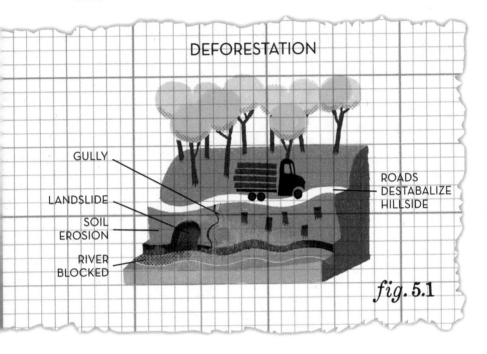

DEFORESTATION

GULLY

LANDSLIDE

SOIL
EROSION

RIVER
BLOCKED

ROADS
DESTABALIZE
HILLSIDE

fig. **5.1**

• • •

RRRRUUUUUHHHHHRRRRR!

The roar of the giant excavator scooping up a massive bucket load of earth rattles the forest.

The Mining Crew boss, wearing a bright orange safety vest, stands next to an **EARTH/HEART** dump truck, yelling through a bullhorn.

"Faster, faster, faster!"

"What's the big hurry?" the excavator driver asks the bucket operator.

"I don't know. But the Big Boss says we got a week to strip out as much coal as we can."

"That's nuts," says the driver.

"Faster, faster, faster!"

The driver shrugs. He positions the excavator for another scoop.

The bucket gouges out another twenty cubic yards of earth.

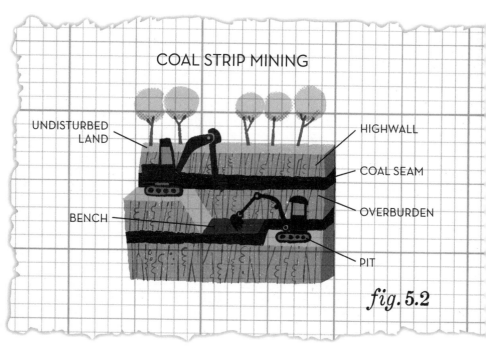

COAL STRIP MINING

UNDISTURBED LAND

HIGHWALL

COAL SEAM

BENCH

OVERBURDEN

PIT

*fig.*5.2

• • •

EEeeeeeeeeeeeeeeeeeeeeeeeeeee! The whine of a huge drill boring through the earth shakes the whole road.

The Drilling Crew boss, wearing a bright orange safety vest, stands next to the **EARTH/HEART** drill truck, yelling through a bullhorn.

"Faster, faster, faster!"

"What's the big rush?" asks one of the drillers.

"No telling. But the Big Boss says we have to tap as much as we can in the next week."

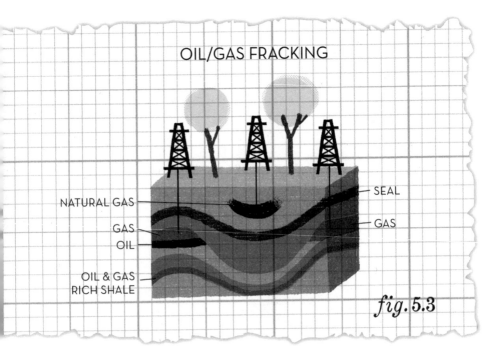

OIL/GAS FRACKING

NATURAL GAS

GAS

OIL

OIL & GAS
RICH SHALE

SEAL

GAS

*fig.*5.3

The drill bit rips through another layer of rock.

"That's crazy," says the one driller.

"Faster, faster, faster!"

The other driller shrugs. He revs up the drill.

And punches another hole deep into the earth.

• • •

A blue plastic bag tumbles across the field and over the fallen oak tree.

A blue plastic bag falls into the trenched earth.

A blue plastic bag spins behind the drilling truck and across the muddy road.

4

FRANK EINSTEIN AND HIS PAL WATSON LUG TWO LARGE CANVAS BAGS of robot parts into Grampa Al's big red barn.

Grampa Al looks up from the mower engine he is fixing.

"Well, hello, Einstein."

"Hello, Einstein," Frank answers absently.

"What genius scheme are you guys cooking up today?"

Frank and Watson drop the bags on the old barn workbench with a noisy metal rattle.

Klink rolls through the double barn doors, carrying a big metal cylinder. He sets it on the workbench, and answers Grampa Al.

"Klank malfunction. We had to disassemble him for transport back here."

Watson rearranges the aluminum-hose-duct arms and vegetable strainer. "Aw, don't say it like that. Klank just had an accident. We can fix him."

Grampa Al wipes the motor oil off his hands and comes over to take a look.

Frank unscrews the access cover to the head port.

Grampa Al leans in and peers over his glasses. "Hmm-mmmm." He clicks the brain gear a few turns. "Uh-huh." He test-spins the balance gyro. "Ah-ha."

Grampa Al shakes his head and gives a low whistle. "Wow. This is a real mess. We may not be able to fix this."

"Exactly," beeps Klink. "As I said earlier."

"Of course we can fix it!" says Frank Einstein, picking a few more shreds of blue plastic out of Klank's brain gear. "We are scientists. That's what we do."

Watson straightens the bent antenna on the robot's vegetable-strainer head.

"We aren't talking about some hunk of junk. We're talking about Klank!"

Grampa Al scratches his head, just like Frank Einstein does when he is thinking. He takes another look inside the clockwork head. "It is our job to try to understand the world. But sometimes we have to realize we can't fix everything."

Grampa Al opens Klank's heart panel and takes a closer look. "Gadzooks! What happened?"

Watson explains, "Up on your land next to the Midville preserve, someone is drilling. And sawing. And digging. And—"

"Klank sucked a plastic bag into his ventilator port," Frank finishes Watson's rambling explanation.

Grampa Al nods.

He resets the power supply.

He reconnects the main-branch crossover cables.

He recleans the microcontroller.

Grampa Al shakes his head. "This is a real soup sandwich. I don't think we will be able to rebuild the same old Klank with what we have on hand."

Frank leans over Grampa Al's shoulder. "What if we

use some of the memory power . . . and cross wire it to the servo-motor?"

"That could work..." says Grampa Al, thinking out loud. "But we don't know how that might affect the self-learning loop."

Klink calculates what might happen. He says one word: "Dangerously."

Watson paces back and forth. "All because of a stupid plastic bag! What was it even doing out in the Midville preserve? That is protected land!" He picks up one of the canvas bags. "Klank could have been saved with a simple invention like this!"

Frank rewires Klank's memory banks. "It's not that simple, Watson."

Watson keeps raging. "Well, it could be. Some of the world's greatest inventions were the most simple. The wheel! The zipper! Toilet paper! We should make something like that to save the world!"

Klink rolls his eye. "And make me a world-class ballerina while you are at it."

Frank finishes the repair as best he can. He and Grampa Al rebuild Klank with farm parts they have, giving Klank new suspension-spring legs, a pitchfork hand, and big rubber tractor-tread feet.

"Well, we are not just going to sit around and watch the world get messed up. Let's do something big to fix it."

Frank closes Klank's heart port and screws it shut.

Grampa Al flips Klank's power switch back on. "Exactly right, Einstein."

Grampa Al points to an old postcard of Albert Einstein tacked up on a barn beam. "It's like the other Al Einstein once said—*The world is a dangerous place to live; not because of the people who are evil, but because of the people who don't do anything about it.*"

Klank's body motor hums.

He lifts his head.

"Hello . . . my name is Klank."

Frank pats Klank's watering-can shoulder and nods.

"Welcome back, Klank. Now let's take care of some important science business."

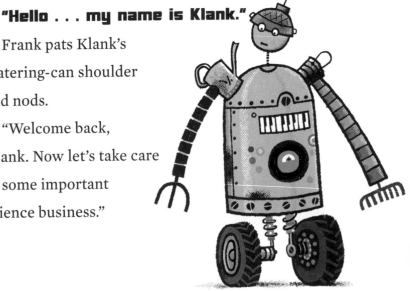

5

FRANK EINSTEIN TACKS UP ONE LAST CHART ON THE IMPROVISED Wall of Science in Grampa Al's barn. "Perfect."

"Aw, dingleberries," says Watson. "I thought we were going to take a vacation. And have our picnic."

"Do you want to be part of the problem? Or part of the solution?" says Frank. "The same carelessness that messed up Klank is messing up the Midville Forest Preserve ... and messing up the whole planet. *And* this fits in perfectly with our next category—planet Earth."

"I know," says Watson. "But I'm hungry."

"HUNGRY?" booms Klank. **"I will get food!"** He jumps to his new tractor-tread feet and rolls for the door.

The one detail that Klank's rewired brain doesn't notice is that the door is closed.

Klank bounces off the barn door with a big metal-on-wood *BOOOOM!*

Frank readjusts Klank's memory setting.

"We will get this right. But first we need background research on planet Earth."

"ᖇᕮᗩᑐᎽ," says Klink. He hands both Frank and Watson Frank's Virtual Reality Eyeballz goggles with blacked-out lenses and tiny wire antennas.

"Klink and I have constructed a virtual world tour of Earth," says Frank. "Put these on. And get ready to travel through Earth science, Frank Einstein style."

Frank and Watson power on the Eyeballz. And he and Watson are instantly in the middle of outer space.

"Whoaaaaaaa!" says Watson.

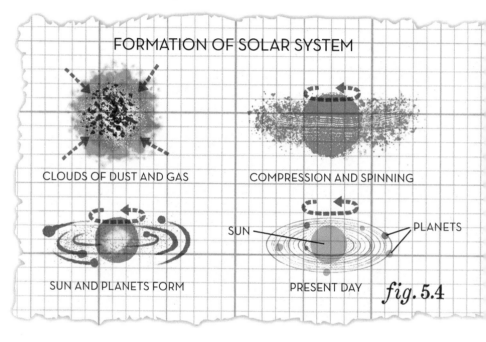

FORMATION OF SOLAR SYSTEM

CLOUDS OF DUST AND GAS

COMPRESSION AND SPINNING

SUN — PLANETS

SUN AND PLANETS FORM

PRESENT DAY *fig.* 5.4

"Five thousand million years ago," says a deep voice, *"this spinning cloud of gas and dust clumped together to form our Sun.*

"Other smaller clouds of gas and dust orbiting around the Sun formed planets.

"One of these planets was Earth."

The space scene shifts. Now Frank and Watson stand on the edge of a desert, next to a strange-looking machine.

"What is this?" asks Watson. "A metal version of a pre-historic shark?"

"Exactly," says Frank. "We made it to look like a megalodon. But mechanical, so it can eat through all the layers of Earth."

Virtual Frank and virtual Watson climb inside. They strap themselves into the pilot and copilot seats behind the Megalodon Driller's crystal-window eyes.

Frank hits the start button and sets the tunneling teeth spinning with a *rrrroooAAARRRRRRR.*

The Megalodon Driller chews through Earth's surface, and starts its dive.

The Megalodon's teeth and lasers cut through the rock and sand.

High-intensity nose beams light its path.

The interior NavMap charts its progress.

Frank punches the Auto Pilot button.

A teeny little guy in a pilot's uniform appears on the dashboard and describes what Frank and Watson are seeing through the Megalodon Driller eye ports.

"The outer, thinnest layer of Earth—the CRUST.

"Mostly rock.

"From eight kilometers to seventy kilometers thick.

"Twenty-two degrees Celsius."

Watson nudges Frank. "How is that big voice coming from that little guy?"

"Nice touch, huh?" answers Frank, admiring his own invention.

The Megalodon's spinning teeth dig into a new, mushy mix.

"We are now in the second layer—the UPPER MANTLE.

"A mix of solid and melted elements and rock. Because it is hot.

"This layer goes from 70 kilometers to 670 kilometers below the surface.

"From 1,400 to 3,000 degrees Celsius.

"We are detecting iron, oxygen, silicon, magnesium, and aluminum."

Frank and Watson watch waves of hot rock and metal wash over the Megalodon.

The chewing teeth hit solid material again.

"The third layer—the INNER MANTLE," the Auto Pilot continues.

"We are 670 kilometers to 2,890 kilometers below the surface.

"Temperature is 3,000 degrees Celsius.

"But now the rock is solid . . . because we are under incredible pressure."

Watson looks around the interior of the Megalodon Driller. "I don't care if it is virtual. This is freaking me out."

The loud, chewing driller goes suddenly quiet and smooth.

"The fourth layer—the OUTER CORE," announces the tiny Auto Pilot.

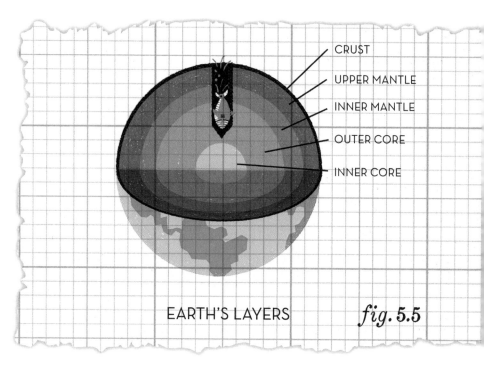

CRUST
UPPER MANTLE
INNER MANTLE
OUTER CORE
INNER CORE

EARTH'S LAYERS

fig. **5.5**

"We are 5,150 kilometers deep.

"Temperatures—4,000 to 6,000 degrees Celsius.

"Iron and nickel are liquid.

"This flows around the inner core, creating Earth's magnetic field."

"How far below the surface?!" asks Watson.

BAM!

The spinning teeth hit a solid block.

"The fifth and innermost layer—the **INNER CORE.**

"A huge metal ball.

"Width is 2,500 kilometers.

"Iron and nickel.

"Temperatures now 5,000 to 6,000 degrees Celsius. But solid because of the pressure."

Frank Einstein turns the Megalodon Driller around. "OK, let's head back home."

The Megalodon hyperspeeds out of the inner core and back through the outer core, the inner mantle, the upper mantle, and into the crust.

Frank scans the NavMap. "We need a good exit." He spots a magma chamber. "Ah, here we go." Frank steers into an underground pool of molten rock.

The Megalodon Driller swims through the chamber, straight up a vent, and flies out of the cone of a lava-spewing volcano.

"Woooo-hooo!" cheers Watson.

The Megalodon Driller lands on a forest floor with a thump.

Frank and Watson pull off their Virtual Reality Eyeballz.

And find themselves standing, a little unsteadily, back in the middle of Grampa Al's barn.

Watson holds his head. "Amazing, Einstein! Truly amazing."

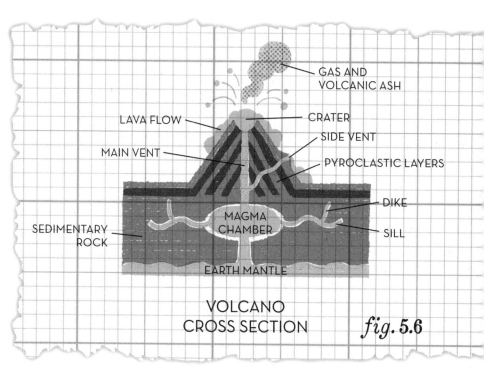

GAS AND VOLCANIC ASH

LAVA FLOW

CRATER

SIDE VENT

MAIN VENT

PYROCLASTIC LAYERS

DIKE

SEDIMENTARY ROCK

MAGMA CHAMBER

SILL

EARTH MANTLE

VOLCANO CROSS SECTION

fig. **5.6**

"No kidding," says Frank. He scans his papers. "Now we have to figure out how Earth *climates* work."

"Oh no," says Watson. "After all that chewing, first we have to figure out how *lunch* works."

"LUNCH?!" booms Klank. He jumps up and rolls for the barn doors. His new memory bank still does not have any information on opening doors.

"Oh boy." says Klink, closing his one eye.

BLAAAAM! Klank bounces off the closed doors.

"Sorry, Klank," says Frank. "We'll have to work on that."

6

A SCRATCHY VOICE CRACKLES OUT OF THE DUSTY SPEAKERS IN THE ceiling of the old Midville Metro movie theater lobby. "OK, **EARTH/HEART** employees. Lunch break is over. Return to your seats for Part Two."

A small crowd of working men and women, wearing blue jeans and bright orange safety vests, shuffles back to the worn red-velvet theater seats.

The lights dim. The silver screen glows with a big blue logo.

Soft, soothing harp music thrums.

The planet Earth logo animates and grows into a spinning globe.

An insistent, professional-radio-sounding voice slowly intones, "Earth.

Our planet. We at **EARTH/HEART , INCORPORATED**, love our planet Earth."

The animation zooms down to ground level, into a lush jungle.

"And we love the fuel Earth gives to us."

The soundtrack suddenly bursts into a cheesy disco beat. Rays of multicolored light flash and spin.

EARTH/HEART, INC. TRAINING FILM, PART 2: FOSSIL FUELS! fills the screen.

A bad Saturday-morning-cartoon animation of a black rock with stick arms and legs and a crazy smile dances onscreen to the disco beat.

The dancing rock stops, spreads his arms, and in a goofy voice blurts, "Well, hello there! I'm Lumpy! The Lump of Coal!"

"Holy smoke!" whispers one of the **EARTH/HEART** employees with FRED written above his shirt pocket.

Lumpy dances a few more jerky steps. "And I am going to tell you all about fossil fuels!—Coal! Oil! Gas!"

"Oh please no," whispers employee Betty sitting next to Fred.

"How Earth made fossil fuels! And how Earth gives fossil fuels to us!"

Betty groans. "Please . . . just shoot me now."

Lumpy dances off to one side of the screen and launches into his lesson.

"Three hundred and fifty million years ago, Earth was *covered* with plants. These plants died, were buried under soil and rock, and got *squashed* for millions of years."

Lumpy dances another two-step.

"Millions of years of heat and pressure squeezed the plant material, made

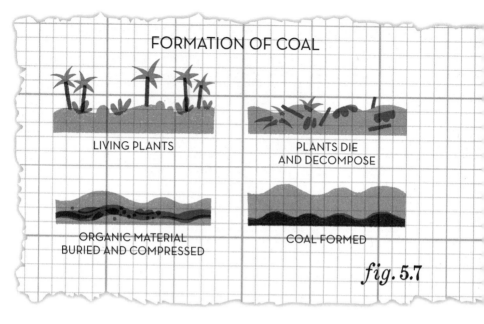

FORMATION OF COAL

LIVING PLANTS

PLANTS DIE
AND DECOMPOSE

ORGANIC MATERIAL
BURIED AND COMPRESSED

COAL FORMED

fig. 5.7

of carbon and hydrogen and oxygen, into almost pure carbon! Or me . . . *coal!*"

"Please make it stop," says Betty. "I promise I will be good."

Fred laughs.

Lumpy does not stop.

"And at the same time, millions of years ago, the tiny plants and animals that lived in the oceans died, and settled on the ocean floor. They were also covered by sediment . . . that became rock."

"The dead plant and animal matter, after millions and millions of years of heat and pressure, breaks down. And turns into natural gas . . . and oil!

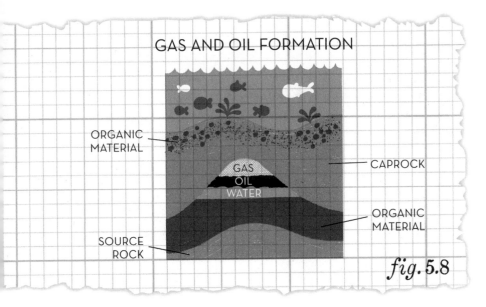

GAS AND OIL FORMATION

ORGANIC MATERIAL

CAPROCK

GAS
OIL
WATER

ORGANIC MATERIAL

SOURCE ROCK

fig. 5.8

"Our other two *fossil fuels!*"

The disco soundtrack turns into a little more of a rap beat.

"No, no, no!" says Fred, guessing what is coming. "Please nooooo—"

But Lumpy doesn't listen. He is a training-film cartoon character. And can't be stopped.

Lumpy breaks into exactly what Fred knew was coming—a terrible half-disco/half-rap fossil fuel song.

"Check, check, check, I am Lumpy the Coal.
Talking 'bout fossil fuel energy is my GOAL!
'Cause can't you see—"

Fred and Betty and most of the other **EARTH/HEART** workers try to cover their eyes and ears.

Lumpy's song goes on for way too long.

It reexplains how coal, oil, and gas come from prehistoric plant and animal life.

It reexplains how that is a "dope fresh thing."

Lumpy finally stops, and puts his stick hands on his coal hips.

"Welp! There you have it, friends! The beauty of fossil fuels!"

Lumpy dances off. The cartoon Earth spins into the **EARTH/HEART** logo and fills the screen.

The soothing harp music returns.

And so does the radio-announcer voice.

"So the next time someone asks you what kind of work you do for **EARTH/HEART , INCORPORATED** . . . tell them you love Earth."

The whole audience of loggers, drillers, and diggers groans.

A loud, piercing bullhorn beep-blasts everyone into silence.

And that same familiar, annoying voice from the lunch announcement blares:

"Now . . . get back to work!"

7

HIGH IN THE TOP OF AN AMERICAN HORNBEAM TREE JUST OUTSIDE the Midville Forest Preserve, Watson holds on to a slim branch with one hand, and a ham and Swiss cheese on pumpernickel bread with mustard sandwich in the other.

"Mmmmphhh rmmm phhmmm mmm, mmm rrr frrr mmm," says Watson through a mouthful of sandwich.

Frank Einstein, wedged comfortably in a fork of the same tree, peers through his special No-Hands Binoculars while eating his crunchy peanut butter and strawberry jelly on white bread sandwich.

"Stop your worrying. This is the perfect spot. One, to find out who is really behind this **EARTH/HEART** company. And two, to be sitting in one of nature's most impressive carbon-removing machines—the tree."

The magnificent tree sways in the breeze.

Watson swallows. Hard. "OK, this is a good spy spot. But do we really need to be up so high?"

Frank Einstein stands up in the top of the tree and looks over the miles of forest and rocks and streams and blue sky. "Yes. Because this is where I do some of my best invention thinking."

Watson takes another bite of his sandwich and nods. He understands. "But I still think the answer could be a really simple invention. Like this."

Watson holds up his one-hand lunch. "Thought up by a British earl in the late 1700s. He didn't want to get up from the table and leave his card game. So he asked for a piece of roast beef between two slices of bread so he could eat and still play cards. The idea caught on. And people started asking for it by using his name—the Earl of Sandwich."

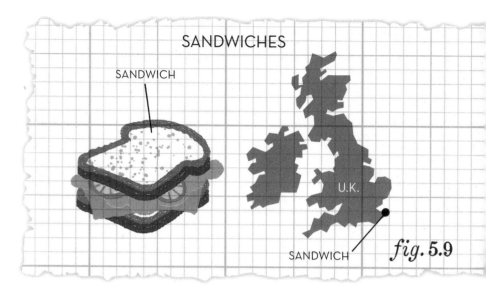

SANDWICHES

SANDWICH

U.K.

SANDWICH

fig. 5.9

Frank laughs. "That is a pretty great invention." Frank looks out over the Midville Forest Preserve. "But I think we can make something huge . . . and impressive."

Weeeeeeeeeeeeeeeeeeeeeeeeeeeeeeee . . .

Chain saws whine. A tree falls.

Raaaaaaaaaaaaaarrrrrrrrrrrrrrrr . . .

Drills roar. The earth shakes.

Brrrrrrrrrrrruuuuuummmmmm . . .

Diggers rumble. A hill disappears.

Frank scans crazy-looking clouds overhead. He scratches his head. "So here is our problem—exactly this kind of human activity is changing the world. Changing the climate. In terrible ways."

Watson finishes his sandwich, and puts his paper trash back in his string bag looped around his belt. "But hasn't Earth's climate always changed?"

"Oh sure," says Frank. "When the dinosaurs were around, it was so warm there were no polar ice caps at all."

"So why worry about things getting a little warmer?"

Frank sways in the treetop. "Earth is warming up way faster than it ever has. And it's being caused mostly by us. By humans producing too much carbon dioxide and other gases that trap heat."

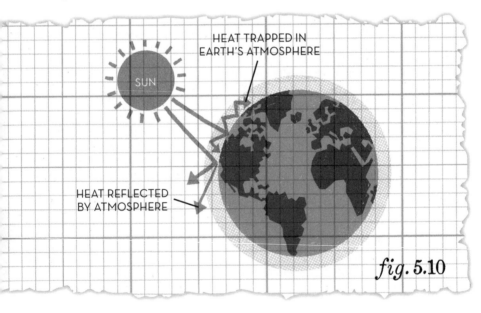

fig. 5.10

"So what? A warmer winter is nicer."

"Nicer? The rise of carbon dioxide in the atmosphere

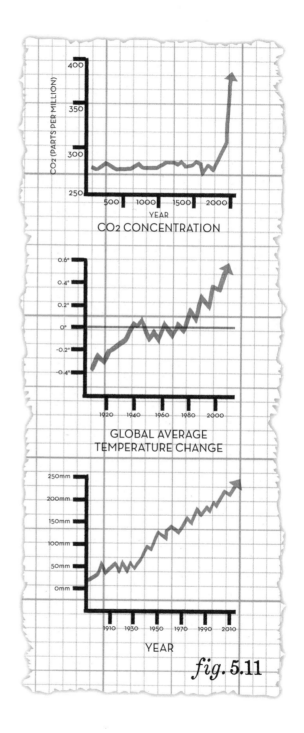

400

350

300

250

CO2 (PARTS PER MILLION)

500   1000   1500   2000
YEAR
CO2 CONCENTRATION

"... has increased the temperature of Earth.

0.6°
0.4°
0.2°
0°
-0.2°
-0.4°

1920   1940   1960   1980   2000
GLOBAL AVERAGE
TEMPERATURE CHANGE

"And it's melting the ice caps, and raising sea levels.

250mm
200mm
150mm
100mm
50mm
0mm

1910   1930   1950   1970   1990   2010
YEAR

fig. 5.11

"Whole cities are going to disappear. Millions of people will lose their homes. Drinking water will be scarce . . ."

Frank looks at the smoke from the saws and drills and diggers below.

"Fossil fuels made a lot of modern progress possible. But now we know that all this carbon burning in coal, gas, and oil is wrecking our planet."

"This is not good," says Watson. "We have to do something."

The saws roar. Another tree falls.

The drills in the distance . . . *WHIRRRRRRRRR.*

"It would be great to make an amazing invention to reverse this global warming." Frank flips his No-Hands Binoculars back down. "But first we have to figure out who is doing this right here. And who exactly do we stop?"

Frank checks his Einstein WristwatchCompassRadar-Tracker. He follows two dots across the map.

"Which is exactly why we have Klink and Klank moving into position."

Swaying in the top of the tree, Watson thinks about who in the world would be nasty enough to be trashing the planet . . . without caring about anyone else.

The answer comes to him instantly.

"Elementary!" says Watson. "Of course. I know *exactly* who is behind this. It's obvious! Follow me!"

Watson climbs down the tree, drops to the ground, hops on his bike, and pedals off in a streak.

"But Watson!" yells Frank. "We can't leave Klink and Klank with no backup!"

But Watson is already down the path.

Frank climbs down, shaking his head. "And besides, it might not be—"

8

TEDISON AND MR. CHIMP.

They sit quietly in the Edison Laboratories Library and Map Room.

T. Edison studies two huge world maps on the long table.

Mr. Chimp studies his book and slurps vegetable lo mein noodles from the end of his chopsticks. He makes a note on his stack of papers.

T. Edison looks at Mr. Chimp's papers. He doesn't see the title **MASTER PLAN.** All he sees is the header on every page: **PRESIDENT MR. CHIMP.**

T. Edison mumbles to himself, but just loud enough for Mr. Chimp (who has very good hearing) to hear.

"... razzle frazzle ... can't believe I made you president ... rumble grumble ..."

Mr. Chimp closes his book.

He leans forward.

"... what was I thinking? ... Why in the world did I ever do that? ..."

Mr. Chimp shakes his head, gives a low growl, and signs:

B   E   C   A   U   S   E

Mr. Chimp growls a bit louder.

I   S   A   V   E   D

Mr. Chimp curls back his lip and bares his teeth at T. Edison.

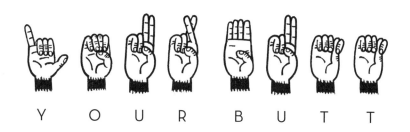

Y   O   U   R   B   U   T   T

T. Edison frowns. He taps his pencil on his map. "I could have taken care of that T. rex no problem. I just wanted you to feel like you were doing something."

Mr. Chimp ignores T. Edison. He has more important things to do.

Mr. Chimp chopsticks another mouthful of lo mein, and adds a doodle to his **MASTER PLAN.**

"And just because you are president doesn't mean you get to do whatever you want."

Mr. Chimp chews his noodles thoughtfully. He has more plans than T. Edison knows. And they are Exactly . . . What. He. Wants.

Mr. Chimp, just to annoy T. Edison, signs in Chinese finger gestures:

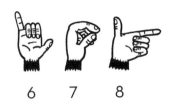

6 7 8

"What are you saying, you annoying ape? I don't speak Chinese! And why are you learning Chinese?"

Mr. Chimp chews.

"And what about those two—"

BAM!

BAM! BAM! BAM!

Something sounding like a baseball bat pounding on the big metal Edison Laboratories doors echoes through the Edison Library.

Mr. Chimp nods, and points his chopsticks at T. Edison.

T. Edison spins the table so it hides the maps, replacing them with a game of snakes and ladders.

BAM!

BAM! BAM! BAM!

Mr. Chimp checks off the first item on his **MASTER PLAN**.

He stands up, straightens his vest, and points to his head as a reminder to T. Edison to be smart.

"Oh, shut up!" growls T. Edison.

9

BAM! BAM! BAM! BAM! WITH HIS BASEBALL BAT, WATSON POUNDS on two giant metal doors of an old brick building across the street from the baseball stadium.

"Open up! I know you are in there! And I know you are behind the whole mess in the Midville preserve."

Frank skids to a stop in front of the building and jumps off his bike. "But Watson—"

BAM! BAM! BAM!

Watson hammers the steel door. "I *know* it's them! I would bet my whole next year's allowance on it. It is *always* them!"

"But Watson—"

BAM!

Frank grabs Watson's bat. A buzzer sounds. The massive steel doors click . . . and then swing open.

In the entrance stands a kid with a terrible haircut, brown wingtip shoes, and a permanent frown. Next to him stands a chimpanzee wearing a white shirt, a tie, and striped pants.

"Yes," confirms Watson. "T. Edison and Mr. Chimp!"

"Wow. That is just brilliant," says T. Edison. "What gave it away? The twelve-foot-tall letters spelling EDISON up there?"

Mr. Chimp gives T. Edison a quick nudge in the ribs.

"Ouch. I mean—it is so nice to see you fellow scientists and inventors."

"You!" says Watson, shaking his finger because Frank has his bat safely behind his back. "You are wrecking our planet."

"Whaaaat?" says T. Edison. "Mr. Chimp and I are here playing snakes and ladders."

Mr. Chimp crosses his powerful chimp arms in front of himself and nods.

"'Wrecking our planet'? What are you talking about?"

"Someone has been drilling, digging, and clear-cutting big pieces of the Midville Forest Preserve," explains Frank Einstein.

"And it's you," adds Watson. "And it has to stop. Because burning coal and gas is warming the whole globe."

Mr. Chimp signs:

S   O   B   A   D

"And don't forget melting the polar ice caps and raising sea levels, too!" says T. Edison.

Watson is shocked. "So you admit it?"

"Oh good heavens no," says T. Edison. "There is absolutely no

proof of any connection between the Edison Company and what is happening out at your precious Midville preserve."

"Oh really?" says Watson. He holds up a plastic bag with the **EARTH/HEART** logo. "And I suppose you don't know anything about this company?"

Mr. Chimp takes the bag, looks at it, and shakes his head no. "Oooo oook."

"The president of the company says, 'No,'" T. Edison translates. "But we would love to help you catch these bad guys. What do they look like?"

"Oooooh," says Watson. "Frank, give me that bat."

"Watson—" says Frank. But he is interrupted by a buzz in his pocket. He checks the mini-beeper.

It's from Klink and Klank.

Backup emergency.

"Uh-oh," says Frank. "Come on, Watson. We have to go."

"Do you have time for a quick game of snakes and ladders?" asks T. Edison.

Watson and Frank hop on their bikes and race back to the preserve as fast as they can, hoping they are not too late.

T. Edison and President Chimp, all smiles, wave good-bye.

TEN MINUTES BEFORE THE BUZZING IN FRANK'S POCKET, KLINK trolls quietly through the underbrush, talking to himself. "I do NOT believe this is the best use of my superior talents. And I most certainly do NOT believe I should be getting dirty."

A low branch of a wild raspberry bush swats Klink's side. "Ouch. That better not leave a mark. I have very sensitive circuits . . ."

The roar of the excavators grows steadily louder.

• • •

Klank's rubber tread clomps over bushes and rocks.

Trying to not forget his mission, he repeats to himself, **"Sneak up on drilling. Take picture. Sneak up on drilling. Take picture. Sneak up on drilling. Take picture."**

The hum of the drilling rig grows steadily louder.

• • •

Inside the flimsy aluminum trailer headquarters, an **EARTH/HEART** crew boss tracks the two blinking dots on his map screen.

"That's it. Closer . . . closer . . . closer . . ."

Both blinking dots reach a red cross on the screen.

The crew boss presses the blue Earth button on his walkie-talkie.

"*Now!*"

• • •

"Oho!" says Klink, spying down on the coal-digging operation.

He raises his camera attachment.

But before he can record any images, a massive mining bucket scoops him up, twirls him over a deep ditch, and dumps him with a metal-bending *CRUNCH!*

• • •

"Ah-ha," says Klank, spying down on the oil-drilling

operation. **"Sneak up. Then . . . uhhh. Sneak up. Then . . . uhhh."**

The drills whine.

". . . take picture!"

Klank raises his camera attachment.

But before he can record anything, a massive drill-pipe hammer smashes down and flattens him with a metal-bending *CRUNCH!*

• • •

A giant bucket loader rumbles through the woods, carrying two crumpled robot heaps. It drives them to the edge of the preserve. And dumps its load in a ditch.

The bucket-loader driver stuffs a plastic bag inside each robot head.

Then punches both Klink's and Klank's backup beepers. And drives off.

Laughing.

II

FRANK EINSTEIN PUSHES AN OLD RED WHEELBARROW, FILLED WITH pieces of bent and twisted metal, into Grampa Al's barn.

Watson, carrying his rope bag filled with more crumpled metal, follows.

"Hello, Einstein," calls Grampa Al, fastening another knot on his Board of Essential Knots. "Check out this fantastic bit of engineering."

"Hello, Einstein," answers Frank glumly. "And I think we are going to need something more fantastic than knots in old rope."

At the sound of Frank's sad response, Grampa Al looks up from his knot board. "What's going on?"

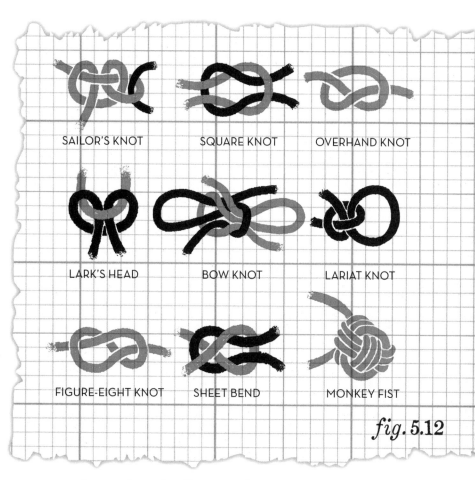

SAILOR'S KNOT SQUARE KNOT OVERHAND KNOT

LARK'S HEAD BOW KNOT LARIAT KNOT

FIGURE-EIGHT KNOT SHEET BEND MONKEY FIST

fig. 5.12

Frank sets the wheelbarrow down.

"More like 'What's getting smashed to *pieces*?'" says Frank. "This is what's left of Klink and Klank."

Grampa Al walks over to inspect the jumble of robot parts. "Heavens to Betsy! What happened?"

"We don't know exactly. But we are pretty sure it wasn't an accident." Frank pulls a plastic bag, with a familiar blue logo, out of a vent piece and holds it up. "A message from the company trashing the preserve."

Watson drops his bag of metal. "And our planet!"

Two brass bells on a wooden box attached to a barn beam ring.

They ring again.

"What the heck is that?" asks Watson. "Your fire alarm?"

Grampa Al lifts up the handset receiver attached to a cord.

"What? You've never seen a real telephone before?"

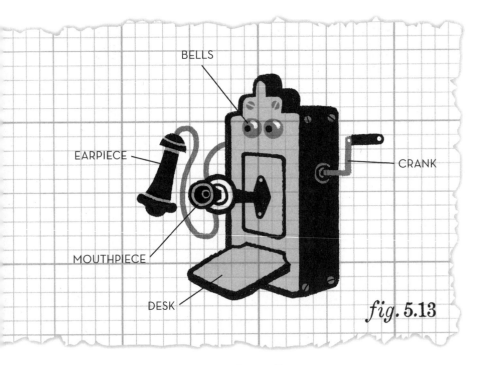

BELLS

EARPIECE

CRANK

MOUTHPIECE

DESK

fig. 5.13

12

MR. CHIMP ROLLS THE DIE ON THE LIBRARY AND MAP TABLE.

He hops his small metal tree token five places from space 16 to space 21.

T. Edison complains, "Oh for goodness' sake!"

Mr. Chimp slides his piece up the ladder on space 16, all the way to space 82, zooming past T. Edison's iron steamroller token.

"Ooook oook," Mr. Chimp teases.

"It's pure luck, I hope you realize."

Mr. Chimp considers the origin of this game in ancient India. He ponders the Indian Hindu philosophy of destiny and desire shaping the outcome of one's life.

T. Edison takes his turn, rolls his die.

"Six! Ha!"

T. Edison smacks his iron steamroller six spaces forward. From 65 to 71.

"*And* I roll again!" T. Edison shakes the die in his hand. "Maybe smart people do get rewarded in this game . . ."

T. Edison rolls a 2.

 He slams his steamroller on 72, lifts it up, then notices the grinning head of the longest snake on the next square, 73.

T. Edison skips 73. He drops his piece down on 74.

Mr. Chimp locks eyes with T. Edison. He holds his stare for one, two, three, four, five, six long seconds. He raises the hair on the back of his neck.

Without breaking his stare, Mr. Chimp reaches over and slides T. Edison's piece back to 73. Back onto the head of the longest snake on the board.

T. Edison looks down at the board. "Oh geez. I must have miscounted."

Mr. Chimp slides T. Edison's steamroller slowly down the snake. From 73 . . . through 68 . . . through 53 . . . 47 . . . 35 . . . 25 . . . 16 . . . 4 . . . 3 . . . 2 . . . and . . . 1.

"Hmmmph," says T. Edison. "All the way back to square one."

Mr. Chimp nods.

"What a stupid game."

Mr. Chimp thinks about destiny and desire.

Mr. Chimp thinks about his recent successes.

Mr. Chimp signs:

And rolls the die . . .

13

THE OLD BARN PHONE'S BRASS BELLS RING AGAIN.

Grampa Al puts the receiver to his ear and speaks into the bell-shaped mouthpiece.

"Hello, Einstein Laboratories and Farm Tool and Tractor Repair."

"Hello, Dad," says a voice from the black plastic receiver.

"Oh, hello, darling. So nice to hear from you! I thought you were out in the middle of the ocean."

"We are. And it is fascinating. So immense. Yet so fragile. Which is what I wanted to tell Frank about. How are he and Watson and my two favorite robots enjoying farm life?"

Grampa Al looks at the motionless pile of bent and broken robot parts.

"Oh great, great . . ." says Grampa Al. "Just hunky-dory. The cat's pajamas."

Frank gives Grampa Al a look.

"Everyone is just ummmmmm . . . really loving it to pieces."

Frank grabs the handset away from Grampa Al before he says any more.

"Hi, Mom."

"Hi, sweetie. Listen, we can't talk long. Because we are in the middle of the Pacific Ocean. But your dad and I have found a problem that desperately needs your inventor help."

Frank scratches his head. "Watson and I are working on a couple of big problems right here . . . but what have you got?"

"Hellllooooooo from the middle of nowhere!" booms a voice from the phone.

Frank holds the handset away from his ear. "Hi, Dad."

"So we are on our way by ship to Hawaii. To check out a new spot for travelallovertheplace.com. And about halfway between California and Hawaii . . . guess what we found?"

Frank sits on a milking stool. "Uhhh, fish?"

"Nope."

"Water?" guesses Watson.

"Well, yes. But, no. It's a strange mess. Right here, the currents of the ocean water swirl around. And that collects all kinds of plastic debris. And it's called the Great Pacific Garbage Patch!"

"Oh yuck," says Watson. "So you are just floating in a giant garbage dump?"

"Not exactly," says Dad Einstein. "But it is an area bigger than Texas! And it has all kinds of big and little pieces of garbage pollution floating at all different depths."

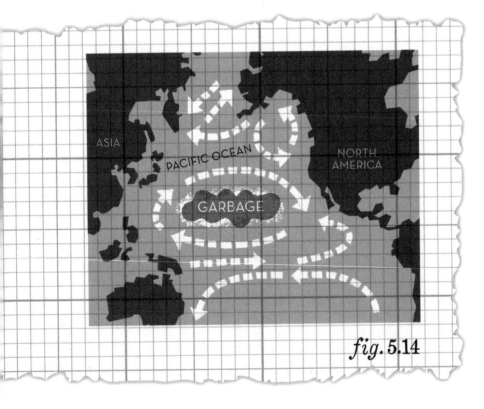

fig. 5.14

Mom takes the phone and adds, "Eighty percent of the garbage is plastic. Because plastic doesn't disintegrate."

Dad chimes in, "And get this . . ."

The old phone suddenly extends a very modern micro-projector, which beams onto the barn wall:

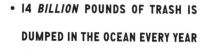

- 14 *BILLION* POUNDS OF TRASH IS DUMPED IN THE OCEAN EVERY YEAR
- AMERICANS GENERATE 10.5 MILLION TONS OF PLASTIC WASTE EVERY YEAR (BUT RECYCLE ONLY 1—2% OF IT)
- THE U.S. USES 100 BILLION PLASTIC BAGS EVERY YEAR
- 1 PLASTIC BAG CAN TAKE 500 YEARS TO DECOMPOSE. SO NEARLY EVERY PIECE OF PLASTIC EVER MADE STILL EXISTS TODAY
- PLASTIC GARBAGE IS KILLING 1 MILLION SEA CREATURES EVERY YEAR

"Oh, man!" says Frank Einstein. "That is terrible."

"Sorry to be such a downer," says Mom Einstein. "But if

anyone can help save the planet, it's you and Watson and your robot pals."

"Thanks, Mom," says Frank Einstein. "We'll see what we can do."

"Love you, sweetie. Say hi to Klink and Klank!"

"OK. Love you."

Frank hangs up the phone.

"What a mess," says Watson. "What are we going to do?"

Frank thinks out loud. "Too much carbon. Too much pollution. Global warming. It's all part of the same giant problem."

Frank looks at the robot parts and the barn full of rakes and hoes and shovels and plows and barrels and drums and old cars and tractors and vacuum-tube radios and belts and fans and an old piano and saws and hoses and axes and hammers and weather balloons and pumps and spark plugs and wires and watering cans and an old pickup truck and glass jars and skeleton keys and rusty locks and horseshoes and nails and leather harnesses and pipes and rope and chains and pulleys and gears and an old tricycle and binoculars and telescopes and screws and springs.

"I've got a few ideas . . ."

14

14 A

"This is it!" says Frank.

He stands proudly in front of his canvas-covered Bio-Action invention, behind Grampa Al's barn.

Watson and a rebuilt Klink (with new tricycle wheel legs) look on.

"The answer to rising CO_2, the greenhouse effect, and air pollution in general!"

"Oh gee, is that all?" says Watson sarcastically.

Frank ignores Watson.

"I give you—**S.U.C.K.**! The **S**uper **U**ltra **C**arbon-absorbing **K**lank!"

Frank whips the canvas off the figure. And reveals... Klank.

Klank blinks his rebuilt robot eyes to adjust them to the change of light.

He turns left, and right, and bows.

"That is just Klank," says Klink. "With radio tubes and an old piano keyboard."

Frank smiles. He plays six notes on Klank's chest keyboard: F, E, D ... F, E, D ...

Klank raises his arms as a series of windshield wipers covered in long pink plastic fibers pops out of them.

Watson and Klink don't know quite what to say.

"You have turned Klank into a fuzzy pink hairball?"

"More like a carbon-absorbing super hero!" says Frank. He cranks the wooden handle on Klank's side.

"Ha!" booms Klank. "That tickles."

Frank flips Klank's new switch labeled EARTH.

Klank's pink plastic branches expand and begin to wave in the air.

"Go, Super Ultra Carbon-absorbing Klank!"

Klank runs toward the woods. He bounces on big tractor-tire feet. He waves his still-sprouting fuzzy pink branches, playing:

Three Blind Mice,

Three Blind Mice.

See how they run.

See how they run.

"My branches absorb one ton of carbon a day."

"Wow," says Watson.

Klink calculates. **"So one million S.U.C.K.s could absorb one million tons of carbon from the atmosphere in one day."**

"Exactly," beams inventor Frank.

"But that is only one percent of global carbon emissions."

"We have to start somewhere," Frank begins to explain, when suddenly—

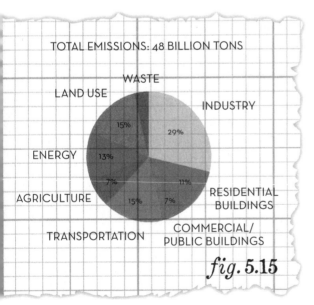

TOTAL EMISSIONS: 48 BILLION TONS

WASTE

LAND USE

INDUSTRY

15%

29%

ENERGY 13%

7%

11%

AGRICULTURE

15%

7%

RESIDENTIAL BUILDINGS

TRANSPORTATION

COMMERCIAL/ PUBLIC BUILDINGS

fig. **5.15**

Klank freezes, and spreads his fuzzy pink carbon-absorbing branches wide.

Klank falls over.

"Rats," says Frank.

"And by the way," says Watson. "That is a terrible name for an invention."

14 B

"OK, this is *really* it!" says Frank.

He stands proudly next to his canvas-covered invention, behind Grampa Al's barn.

Watson and Klink look on.

"This will slow the greenhouse effect, and cool global warming for sure."

"Why do you always do this with the canvas?" asks Watson.

"It is supposed to be dramatic."

"Oh," says Klink.

"I give you—the **S**ulfur **A**ction **D**istribution cannon!"

Frank whips the canvas off the figure. And reveals . . . Klank again. This time with a milk-can body and two long metal tubes, studded with shower nozzles, for arms.

Klank waves his arm cannons.

Watson and Klink jump out of the way.

"Be careful where you are pointing those cannons!" Watson calls from behind a bale of hay.

"Why would you give Klank cannons?" asks Klink.

"In 1991, a volcano in the Philippines exploded..." Frank Einstein explains.

"Yes, the effects of the eruption affected the entire Earth," Klink confirms. "Ten billion tons of magma were ejected. Twenty billion tons of SO_2— sulfur dioxide— were ejected. In the months following the eruption, the ejected material formed a global layer of sulfuric-acid haze. Over the next two years, global temperatures dropped by about 0.5 degrees Celsius, and ozone depletion temporarily decreased substantially."

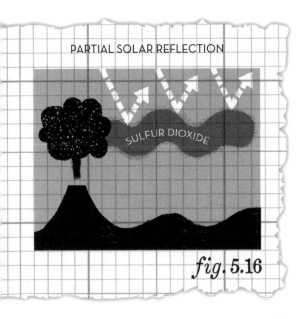

PARTIAL SOLAR REFLECTION

SULFUR DIOXIDE

fig. 5.16

"So?" says Watson.

Frank smiles. "So what if we imitated that eruption? And put sulfur particles in the stratosphere?"

"Sunlight would reflect off the sulfur particles, cooling Earth," figures Klink.

Frank plays a new se-
ries of notes on Klank's
chest piano keys.

Frank cranks the handle on Klank's side. He flips Klank's **EARTH** switch.

A back panel on Klank's new milk-can body flaps open. A weather balloon unfurls, fills with helium, and rises over Klank's head.

Klank floats up.

Frank holds on to him with a rope and harness.

Klank drifts over Grampa Al's hayfield. He sprays a mist out his shower-nozzle arm cannons.

"'All around the Earth's stratosphere . . .'" sings the floating Klank, happily building a dense cloud over the field.

"Look at that!" cheers Frank. "He's shading the whole field. And cooling it, too."

Watson admires the sun-stopping cloud. "Very impressive. But what is that terrible smell?"

"Ah, just a little SO_2," says Frank. "Sulfur dioxide."

"And why are those plants wilting?"

"Other effects of SO_2 include damage to plant life," beeps Klink.

"*Ack, ack ack!*" Watson coughs. "And why am I having trouble breathing?"

"Some individuals are sensitive to SO_2. Breathing difficulties, headache, and nausea may occur."

Frank's eyes water. He coughs, too. "For the good of the planet."

"Any tig edlse?" wheezes Watson, holding his nose.

Klank takes a wide turn overhead.

"Sulfur dioxide may also damage fabric, paper, leather, paints, marble, slate, cement, rocks, and electrical components," reports Klink.

Right on cue, Klank's electrical spraying components start sparking.

"Pop goes the—"

Klank sputters, jets, and starts cartwheeling through the sky.

Frank can't hold the thrashing robot on the end of the rope. He quickly ties it to the fence.

"EEEEEEEEEEE!" beeps out-of-control Klank.

He spins, sprays, plunges straight for Earth . . . and crashes with a hollow *POOOOM!* in a lucky-for-Klank haystack.

"Other side effects of SO_2 distribution are unpredictable . . ."

"And by duh way . . ." adds Watson, still plugging his nose, "S.A.D. is another terrible name for an invention."

"OK, this is really, really it!" says Frank.

He stands proudly inside Grampa Al's pasture.

Klank, newly fitted with one vacuum-hose arm and one metal-scoop hand, looking very nervous for a robot, stands next to Grampa Al's cow, Mildred.

"Now *this* is the Einstein invention guaranteed to save the planet."

"What, no canvas?" asks Watson.

Frank gives Watson a look. "So carbon dioxide is a big problem warming the atmosphere. But did you know that methane gas is twenty-five times more harmful than CO_2?"

"I did not."

"And do you know where a big percent of that global methane gas comes from?"

"No," says Watson.

"Moooooooo," says Mildred.

"Yes," says Frank. "From the burps and farts of cows."

Watson stares at Frank, trying not to laugh. "You are kidding."

"I am not kidding," answers Frank. "So if we get rid of this methane, we reduce greenhouse gases."

Watson raises one eyebrow, still not sure about this whole idea. "But how do you do that? You can't stop cows from burping and farting."

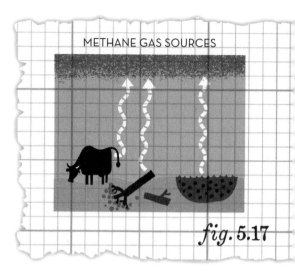

METHANE GAS SOURCES

fig. **5.17**

"No," says Frank.

"But here is what we *can* do. We can use my invention."

"Mooooooo," says Mildred.

Now Klank looks completely uncomfortable.

"Let me guess," says Klink. "Is it named P.O.O.P.?"

"Don't be ridiculous," says Frank. "That is a terrible name for an invention. This is the **M**ethane **O**rganizing **R**ecycling **E**ngine **D**evice **O**f **O**rganic **D**ynamics **O**ccurring **O**utside!"

It takes a minute for Watson to figure out the acronym.

"M.O.R.E. D.O.O. D.O.O.?"

"The demonstration!" says Frank.

Frank feeds a handful of grain to Mildred. She chews.

"We can't eliminate the methane," says Frank.

"But you could DOO DOO a much better job of collecting it and using it," says Klink.

Watson looks at Klink.

"Did you just make a joke?"

Klank frowns. **"That is not funny."**

It looks like Klink smiles.

Frank cranks the handle on Klank's side. He activates Klank's M.O.R.E. D.O.O. D.O.O. by play- ing a new sequence on Klank's piano keys.

Klank's vacuum-hose arm and metal-scoop hand extend.

Frank feeds Mildred another handful of grain. Mildred chews and swallows.

Klank's processing light blinks red. His piano keys play *". . . and on his farm he had a—"*

Mildred sniffs, snorts, and then belches: *"BUUUURP!"*

Klank's M.O.R.E. D.O.O. D.O.O. vacuum arm inhales the burped methane gas and stores it inside Klank's holding tank.

Mildred snorts. She lifts her tail.

Klank's keyboard plays, *". . . with a moo moo here—"*

Mildred excretes a steaming load of manure.

Klank holds out his M.O.R.E. D.O.O. D.O.O. scoop arm and catches the pile of hot cow poop.

Klank closes his eyes, and drops the dung into his collection slot.

Klank's processor light blinks yellow. His keyboard plays, ". . . *and a moo moo there. Here a moo, there a moo, everywhere a moo moo* . . ."

Klank processes the cow poop into gas. Klank's processing light blinks green.

"Aha!" says Frank. He pulls Klank's gas-release finger.

It hisses methane gas. Which lights on fire with blue flame.

"Success!" cheers Frank. "*And* we have made a new, usable source of heating and cooking power!"

"That's great," says Watson. "But how are we ever going to build enough ... um ... M.O.R.E. D.O.O. D.O.O. machines to follow every cow and goat and sheep around?"

"Ninety million tons of methane a year," calculates Klink, "would require at least forty million M.O.R.E. D.O.O. D.O.O.s."

Klank makes a sad sound.

"Awww shoot," says Frank. "You are right. That is too much robot-building. We would end up using more energy, and producing more CO_2, than we would collect."

Klank tries to shake the last of the cow poop off his scoop.

"OH, NOW YOU FIGURE THAT OUT."

"Sorry, Klank."

"E—I—E—I—O," sighs Klank.

Mildred agrees with a sympathetic methane *poot*.

15

MR. CHIMP SITS IN HIS NEW CHAIR, BEHIND HIS NEW DESK, IN his new office.

He adjusts his tie.

He taps his shoes.

He checks the numbers on his ChimpEdison spreadsheet.

He types a quick e-mail to all ChimpEdison managers.

He orders dinner from the ChimpEdison cafeteria. His favorite—Wild Weed and Nut Salad, with Termites.

Mr. Chimp closes his laptop, leans back, and crosses his feet on his desk.

He looks out his corner-office windows at Midville spread out below him.

He is President Chimp.

He is a success.

Mr. Chimp hoots a small "ooook" that no one hears.

The golden evening sun lights the tops of the buildings and trees with a beautiful glow.

Mr. Chimp thinks, *What a wonderful—OWWW!* A sharp pinch cramps his left big toe. Mr. Chimp pulls off his shoe. He hops around his office, stomping the pain out of his toe.

Mr. Chimp puts his shoe back on, carefully ties it, and gets back to work.

He stacks his papers. He shelves his books.

Mr. Chimp opens an old file box. It is full of photos and newspaper clippings. Mr. Chimp sits on the edge of his desk. He had forgotten all about these. He leafs through:

**GREAT-GRANDPA CHIMP
IN HOLLYWOOD**

**GRANDPA CHIMP IN
THE SPACE PROGRAM**

**GRANDMA CHIMP
IN THE NEWS**

**DAD CHIMP
IN RESEARCH**

Mr. Chimp quickly closes the box and shoves it on the shelf next to his copy of *Beyond Good and Evil*.

Mr. Chimp feels another pinch. But not in his shoe. In his animal heart.

Mr. Chimp feels a missing. A something not there. He shakes his head.

A rumble rattles the old factory windows.

Mr. Chimp looks up.

A line of dark storm clouds moving in from the west. Trees swaying. The distant forest of the preserve. Trees. Trees. Trees . . .

Mr. Chimp thinks for a second. Or actually—doesn't think. He acts.

Mr. Chimp bolts out of his office, hop-swing-slides down the back stairs. He jumps on his motorcycle and races to the Midville preserve.

Streets, sidewalks, people blur.

Mr. Chimp jumps off his motorcycle and knuckle-runs through the woods like the devil is chasing him. Bushes thrash, dust whirls in the quickening winds of the approaching storm.

Mr. Chimp kicks off his shoes. He leaps to grab his favorite tree. He scrambles up the trunk, swinging from branch to branch, hand over hand, until he lands with a thump in the woven-branch center of his most favorite tree-house nest.

The towering oak sways majestically. Clouds race overhead.

Mr. Chimp pulls off his tie.

Mr. Chimp rips off his vest.

Mr. Chimp raises his arms and yells the most confused, happy, sad, wild *OOOOOOOOK* you have ever heard.

16

TEDISON HUNCHES OVER THE CHARTS ON HIS DESK.

He studies the latest news on EdisonChimp production.

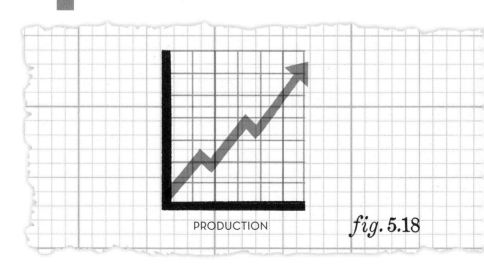

PRODUCTION

fig. 5.18

He checks the progress of EdisonChimp inventions.

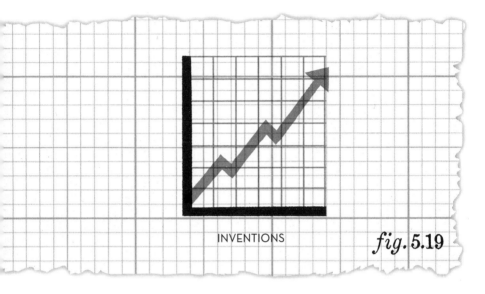

INVENTIONS

fig. **5.19**

Double-checks the numbers on EdisonChimp profits.

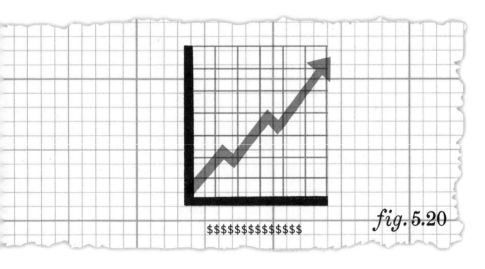

$$$$$$$$$$$$$$$

fig. **5.20**

T. Edison jumps up on his desk. He raises his arms and squeaks the weirdest "Yesssssss!" yell you have ever heard.

And then he gives his awkward version of a pro-athlete fist pump.

Which makes the whole scene all that much creepier.

T. Edison stands on top of his desk, hands on hips.

He is a success.

No one can take that from him.

T. Edison looks out his corner-office windows at all of Midville spread out below him, and happily mutters, "Idiots."

T. Edison notices that his portrait is hanging a bit crooked.

He jumps down from his desk and straightens it, admires it.

A rumble rattles the old factory windows.

T. Edison looks up.

He spots a small black ant on the windowsill outside.

"Now, how did you get all the way up here, little ant?"

T. Edison opens the window.

"Twelve stories high? That is like *miles* for you."

T. Edison reaches down, bends a stubby finger close to the ant, and flicks him off the ledge. He watches the ant

spin, tumble, fall away to nothing. Then he stalks over to his phone, jabs a button, and barks into it, "Miss Poz! We have an ant problem! Call the exterminator! What? Yes—*now!*"

Thunder from the moving storm rumbles closer, louder.

A gust of wind blows in the open window and blasts through T. Edison's office in a mini-tornado.

T. Edison slams his window shut.

But not before the wind has scattered charts, papers, pictures, and a stack of plastic bags with a very distinct blue logo.

17

WHAT A MESS."

Frank, Watson, and Grampa Al sit out back at the picnic table.

"Oh no it's not," says Grampa Al, still messing around with his rope and knots. "It's a sheepshank. Simple . . . and perfectly designed to take up slack."

Frank, slumped over, holds his head in both hands. "No, I mean this whole

giant mess of Earth being wrecked, and none of my inventions helping at all."

Grampa Al drops his knot, and serves Frank an ear of fresh-roasted sweet corn.

"Don't be so hard on yourself, Einstein.

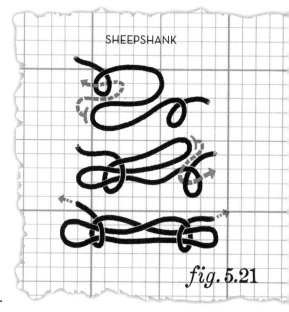

SHEEPSHANK

fig. 5.21

Remember, our other favorite Einstein said, 'A person who never made a mistake never tried anything new.' And besides— this corn is delicious!"

Watson helps himself to more tomatoes, cucumbers, and baby lettuce. "No kidding. Nothing like fresh from the garden. Fresh from the earth."

The light of the setting sun paints the fields and trees in a golden light.

But Frank is still crushed. He picks up his fork and pushes Grampa Al's famous potato salad around on his plate.

"How did we go so wrong? Nothing worked. And we aren't any closer to saving the preserve. Or our planet."

Grampa Al finishes off one more ear of corn, then starts on his cherry pie.

"Maybe you didn't go so wrong. Maybe the world has to catch up with you. Some of the best scientific breakthroughs were called crazy when they first came out."

Frank rests his chin on one hand and frowns.

Watson eyes Frank's untouched cherry pie. He pulls his latest simple invention out of his pocket—the telescoping fork.

Grampa waves his hands in the air and continues. "Like the idea that Earth is round! Or the hypothesis that all the planets revolve around the sun! Or that the continents move."

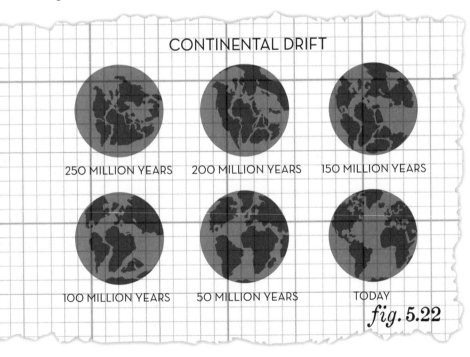

CONTINENTAL DRIFT

250 MILLION YEARS   200 MILLION YEARS   150 MILLION YEARS

100 MILLION YEARS   50 MILLION YEARS   TODAY

fig. 5.22

Watson extends the antenna soldered onto the fork handle. He sneaks it across the picnic table and forks a piece of Frank's pie.

Frank doesn't even notice.

Watson inhales the bite of pie, and realizes Frank is really out of it.

The wind picks up, ruffling the grasses and the tablecloth.

"Or one of my favorites . . ."

A small black ant drops on the table. Grampa Al notices. He keeps talking, but reaches down with one finger and gives the ant a crumb of pie.

". . . that scientists are still debating. About the whole Earth. Called the Gaia theory."

The ant picks up the piece of piecrust that's almost the same size as he is, and walks off.

Frank looks up, still feeling terrible, but always interested.

"It's the idea that all living things on Earth, and Earth itself, are one giant connected SUPERorganism. That regulates itself."

Thunder rumbles. A front of dark clouds moves in from the west.

Watson licks his fork clean of every last bit of sweet

cherry pie. "Whaaaaat? So plants and animals and ants and people and weather and everything are all one thing?"

Grampa Al nods. "Abso-toot-ly."

Frank perks up a bit. "But what do you mean: it 'regulates itself'?"

Grampa Al picks up another piece of his rope and starts tying another knot as he explains. "The system of living and nonliving things maintains the conditions to support life. Like raising and lowering its temperature, its oxygen level . . ."

Frank's mind expands with this Gaia thought. "So if Earth was a person, we humans would be like the worst cold virus."

Grampa Al laughs. "I never thought of it that way . . . but yes!"

Thunder rumbles louder now.

Watson, the weather geek, eyeballs the clouds and identifies them. "Cumulonimbus. Serious storm clouds."

The wind rises.

The trees shake.

Grampa Al finishes his knot and holds it up for inspection. Monkey's Fist. Designed to make the end of a rope easier to throw. Simple. Perfect. He looks up at the approaching

clouds. "This is look-
ing like it might be
a real doozy. Let's
get inside and batten
down the hatches."

Grampa Al pockets
his rope and knots and
feels Frank's forehead.

"And let's get you
some R and R. You are
feeling fever hot."

The advancing
clouds blot out the last
of the sun.

A sizzling bolt of
lightning unleashes a
wicked crack smash of
thunder.

The first few drops
of rain splatter the table.

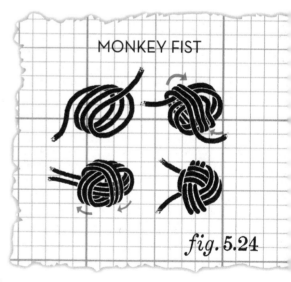

CLOUDS

CIRRUS

CUMULONIMBUS

CIRROCUMULUS

ALTOCUMULUS

CUMULUS

STRATOCUMULUS

fig. **5.23**

MONKEY FIST

fig. **5.24**

The guys grab plates and utensils and run for the farmhouse as the storm hits hard.

18

THE HIGH-PRECIPITATION SUPERCELL THUNDERSTORM, TOWERING ten miles high and spreading twenty miles across, explodes over Midville County with unbelievable force.

Warm air from the east rises into a cloud, carrying moisture up.

Cool air from the west pushes down, condensing moisture into water droplets.

The water droplets fall and smash together to form larger and heavier raindrops.

The falling rain drags the surrounding air with it, creating strong downdraft winds.

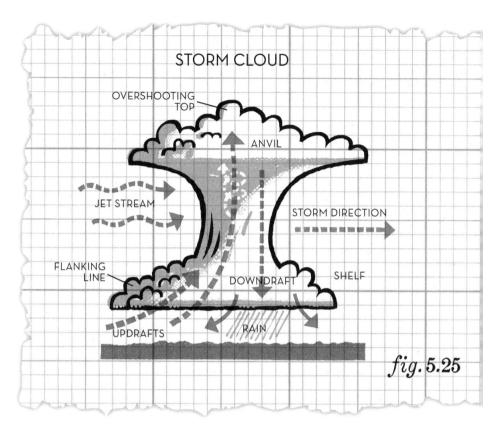

STORM CLOUD

OVERSHOOTING TOP

ANVIL

JET STREAM

STORM DIRECTION

FLANKING LINE

SHELF

DOWNDRAFT

UPDRAFTS

RAIN

fig. 5.25

Lightning flashes. Thunder cracks. An old dead maple tree catches fire. The nearby field erupts in a wall of wildfire.

The ferocious downdraft wind knocks over a whole stand of fifty-year-old maple trees. Seventy-five-mile-per-hour winds flip a row of camping trailers and flatten a row of rickety wooden buildings.

The sudden deluge of rain fills the stream to overflowing. A muddy torrent of sticks, mud, boulders, and water smashes down bridges, swallows up homes. A field of corn, a row of parked cars, the entire side of a hill are all washed away in a flash flood.

The storm moves slowly from west to east—a collision of hot and cool, low-pressure and high-pressure air.

But also an angry giant, throwing fire bolts, smashing with wind, stomping with water all in its path.

19

RAIN HAMMERS THE METAL ROOF.

A blue-white flash of lightning illuminates Klink and Klank, sitting side by side in the driest spot of the old barn—the horse stalls.

Klank stretches out a beat-up ax-handle leg.

Klink flexes his squeaky barn-door-hinge elbow, closes his webcam eye.

Freight-train-loud wind roars through the cracks in the barn walls.

A *SMAAAAASH CRAAAACK!* peal of thunder rocks the whole world.

Klank butt-jumps sideways, closer to Klink.

"Klink," says Klank.

Klink opens his eye. "What?"

"Are you ever afraid?"

Klink pretends to think about this for three seconds, because he knows this makes Klank feel better. "No. Because we are robots. We are never afraid. Or mad. Or sad."

Klank nods his dented vegetable-strainer head. **"Yeah. That is what I thought."**

The storm wind blasts open the hayloft shutter with a mad *BAAAAAM!*

"YIIIIIKES!" Klank wraps Klink in both his irrigation-hose arms.

Klink hands Klank his stuffed teddy bear.

Klank unwraps his arms, strokes the soft fur, and rocks back and forth.

"Now power down, and stop worrying," says Klink.

"OK," says Klank. He pats his teddy bear, rocking it in his arms.

The storm howls and rages and shakes the whole barn. Lightning flashes. Thunder crashes.

Klank tries to power down and stop worrying.

But he can't stop the thinking and the feeling . . . that this is the end of the world.

"Klink?"

Klink does not open his eye. "I am not answering you."

"You just did."

WHOOOOOOOOOOOO! The wind howls and blows through the stalls.

"Oh, for goodness' sake. What?"

Klank pats his teddy bear more slowly. **"Why are we here?"**

This time Klink doesn't wait three seconds. He instantly answers, "Because this is both the driest spot in the barn to protect our electronics . . . and it is closest to the power outlet."

The rain slows, then hammers even harder on the creaking roof.

Klank, now more upset, pets his teddy bear faster. Harder.

"Noooo. I mean why are we *here?* In this world?" He pats his teddy bear. **"What are we doing? What is our dream?"**

Klink blinks. For the first time in his robot life, he doesn't have an answer.

"I do not think this is a good question for a robot to answer. It can only lead to more questions. That cannot be answered."

A blast of downdraft air suddenly blows open the barn window. Lightning explodes. Thunder cracks. The rain splashes in.

Klank jumps . . . and rips the head of his teddy bear right off.

Klink closes and bolts the window against the storm.

He wheels back to Klank, standing frozen-still in the stall.

Klink knows what he has to do.

He sits Klank down gently.

And in the middle of the crashing storm howling all around them, he reaches behind Klank's head, and powers him . . . OFF.

20

RAIN HAMMERS THE METAL ROOF.

Crashing thunder rattles the night.

Fierce winds scream like mad, wild animals and tear at the farmhouse.

Frank Einstein, fever hot, doesn't hear any of it.

Frank Einstein, fever hot, sleeps and worries and dreams.

A vast cloud of deep-space gas spins, spirals, forms a solid orb.

A planet.

Deep blue water covers most of the planet. Lush green jungles and forests cover the land. A layer of gases wraps and cushions the spinning globe.

Mountains rise and fall and split.

Huge pieces of land, continents, driven by currents deep below the planet's surface, drift apart.

The oceans teem with crazy fish life.

Insects, birds, and animals swarm the land.

A field. A garden.

An ear of corn pops out of the rich black soil. He shakes the dirt out of his corn-silk hair and dances a little jig.

"Ahhhhhh . . . earth, water, sun, and air!"

Lady Tomato drops off a vine and joins Mr. Corn.

"Juuuust right."

"Thanks, Gaia!"

Zoom out into space.

Earth nods, and gives a wink.

A tiny black speck appears on the planet.

It quickly turns to more specks, a stain, a rash.

The dark rash spreads across the land, clouds the air, fouls the oceans.

Earth hacks and coughs.

Earth spins, hot and feverish.

Earth wobbles.

A piece of rope snakes through outer space. It loops itself into a perfect lark's head knot around Earth. The knot tightens. Earth sneezes.

The black rash flies off into space.

"Simple," says Watson from somewhere, everywhere. "Simple."

Earth, rid of its bug, sighs.

. . .

Dreaming, Frank zooms in on the teeny specks that made the rash.

A virus?

A worm?

No, the specks are humans.

Every one of the millions—human.

Dreaming Frank looks closer.

And every one of the humans has the face of . . . Frank Einstein.

. . .

Frank sits bolt upright in bed.

Rain hammers on the farmhouse roof.

Thunder crashes. The winds still howl.

. . .

Frank scratches his head

"This gives me an idea . . ."

Frank Einstein jumps out of bed, runs down to the kitchen, and finds what he is looking for—a coil of rope.

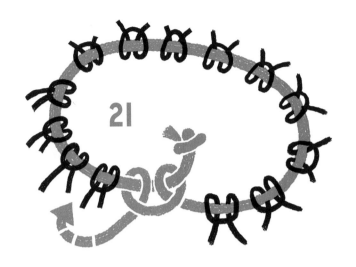

21

FRANK EINSTEIN, STILL IN HIS PAJAMAS, BENDS OVER THE KITCHEN table.

With the thunderstorm crashing around him, he works on his new invention with only his hands, and one idea.

No robots.

No complicated equations.

No tricky mechanics.

No detailed instruction.

Just the rope, a few knots,

. . . and one blazingly simple idea.

Frank works.

The storm blows itself out.

Morning.

First faint light of dawn.

An absolutely clear blue sky.

Birdsong.

Frank holds up his invention.

The most amazing, beautiful, and ultimate Bio-Action Gizmo to save the planet.

But now, how to activate the invention?

Frank sits. Frank scratches his head. Frank thinks.

Frank knows what they have to do.

He wakes up Watson.

They run to the barn to get Klink and Klank . . . and to save the world.

22

SUNRISE IN THE MIDVILLE PRESERVE.

A red-winged blackbird sings.

One bright, puffy white cloud sails across the intensely blue sky.

A gentle morning breeze, smelling of fresh pine, waves the trees.

But the Midville preserve looks like the site of a massive battle:

Full-grown trees, splintered and snapped in half.

Gigantic boulders smashed into the hillside.

Scars of bare earth, exposed by landslides along the stream.

The once-rolling grassy field now torn by a jagged ditch.

A tangle of trucks and drill rigs crumpled and tossed like a ball of aluminum foil.

Two small figures walk through the destruction. One stomping along in oversize black rubber boots, leaving wet oversize footprints in the fresh earth.

The other, barefoot, hop-walking carefully over the trashed land, leaving barely a trace of having stepped there.

"How did this happen?!" screeches the kid in the large boots and bad haircut.

The barefoot chimpanzee in the dirty vest and crooked tie looks at the clueless kid. He thinks about trying to explain his thoughts on nature, fate, and karma. But he decides it isn't worth the time or trouble, and signs:

S   N   A   K   E

T. Edison has no idea what Mr. Chimp is telling him. And he doesn't really care. He walks over to the pile of twisted construction parts. He kicks a bent drill-rig support. And continues his rant.

"This is terrible! Terrible for business. I want more, more, more! Cutting, drilling, mining. I want up, up, up on my charts! Not this stupid storm down, down, down."

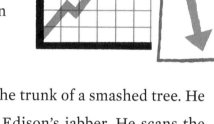

Mr. Chimp hops up on the trunk of a smashed tree. He doesn't hear a word of T. Edison's jabber. He scans the forest ahead, looking for his tree, hoping his tree is safe.

T. Edison stomps, and Mr. Chimp hops deeper into the woods.

Earth, as always, spins, making the sun appear to rise higher in the sky.

FRANK EINSTEIN AND PAL WATSON HEAVE UP THE WOOD-PLANK BARN latch, push open the big double doors.

"Klink! Klank!" calls Frank. "Rise and shine!"

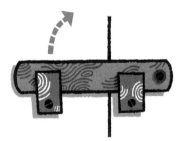

He lifts a canvas-wrapped package. "We have the answer—the most fantastic, powerful, amazing, and instantly effective **BIO-ACTION GIZMO**!"

Watson chimes in. "And we know exactly where to use it. And whose butt we are going to—Ohhhh."

Watson is the first to spot Klank. Sprawled awkwardly on his side. Motionless.

Watson runs over to Klank. Kneels down. Lifts his dented vegetable-strainer head. Holds him.

"Klank?"

Nothing.

No response.

Klink rolls around the corner of the horse stall. He is not the same Klink. Something is different about him.

Frank rests a hand on Klink's power-vac shoulder. "What happened?"

Klink shakes his glass-dome head. "I had to do it. His heart was too big. His head too . . ." Klink's voice trails off.

Watson looks from Klink to the dead-still Klank. "Whaaaaaat?"

He is suddenly horrified.

Frank gives Klink a pat. "You had to do it. His heart *was* too big."

Watson jumps up, runs over, and grabs Frank. "Wait, wait, wait. What are you saying? Klank was too big-hearted? That's crazy! He was the nicest person that ever lived!"

Frank gives Watson a weird look.

"I mean—even if he was a robot."

"AWWWWWWWWWW."

Watson, thinking about Klank lost forever, tears up.

"He did everything for us. He sacrificed himself. He saved our lives. He let you mess him up for all your inventions . . ."

Klank sits up. **"And he even touched cow poop for you."**

"Yeah," says sad Watson. "And he even touched—Hey! What?!"

Watson turns around and sees Klank sitting up. And perfectly fine. Though maybe looking a bit different, too.

Watson jumps like he is seeing a ghost. Then runs to wrap Klank in one of his own HugMeMonkey! heart hugs.

"Klank! You're alive!"

"Of course he is," says Frank. "What did you think? He was dead? Klink and I have been searching for stronger heart-drive pieces for Klank for months."

"I turned Klank off," says Klink. **"Then installed tractor pistons. As we discussed. And a few extras."**

"Oh yeah," says Watson. "I totally knew that."

Klank stands up and thumps his patched metal trashcan chest. **"Strong like tractor! And look at this!"**

Klank pulls back his thumb, and with a deafening roar starts his new chain-saw arm.

"WOW!" Watson yells over the din.

Klank flips his thumb and shuts off his chain-saw arm.

"And Klink, have you been working out?"

It must be a trick of sunlight. Because Klink is a robot. But for a second, it looks like he is blushing.

"Yes. I calculated that more power might be necessary."

Frank smiles. "As Grampa Al would say—Abso-toot-ly Fan. Tas. Tic." Frank picks up his package. "Now, let's roll!

Time to hit the bad guys trashing our Earth. And unleash the best world-changing invention ever. The **BIO-ACTION GIZMO!**"

"**Whoop whoop. Bomp bomp,**" beeps Klank, waving his chain-saw arm.

"**Most certainly,**" beeps Klink, swinging his sledge-hammers.

And the two guys and two robots charge out of the barn.

24

THE RED-WINGED BLACKBIRD PERCHES SILENTLY ON THE STEM OF a broken cattail.

The single white cloud has disappeared.

The two guys and two robots pick their way carefully through the scene of destruction.

Klank chainsaws a downed tree blocking the path.

Frank continues his explanation.

". . . by adding up all those ways you use energy and add greenhouse gases to the

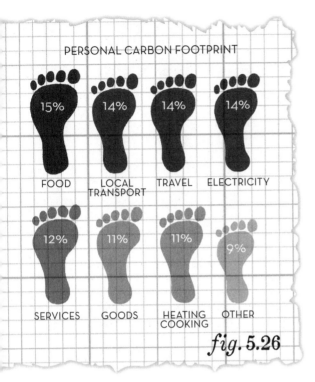

PERSONAL CARBON FOOTPRINT

15%	14%	14%	14%
FOOD	LOCAL TRANSPORT	TRAVEL	ELECTRICITY

12%	11%	11%	9%
SERVICES	GOODS	HEATING COOKING	OTHER

fig. **5.26**

atmosphere, that gives you what is called your carbon footprint."

Watson pushes through a pile of brush. "So stuff like turning on lights, and riding in cars, and buying food?"

"Exactly," says Frank.

"The average American produces twenty *tons* of carbon every year!"

The Einstein team winds through the trashed fields and shattered forests.

Klink clears the way, sledgehammer pounding a granite boulder to gravel.

"And so your plastic footprint is the same kind of measurement," explains Frank.

"All the plastic stuff a person throws out into the world in one year?"

"Yep. Plastic bottles, caps, cups, forks, shoes, straws. Plastic bags especially! Every person throws away three hundred plastic bags a year. They use it for an average of twelve minutes. And it takes 500 years to disintegrate!"

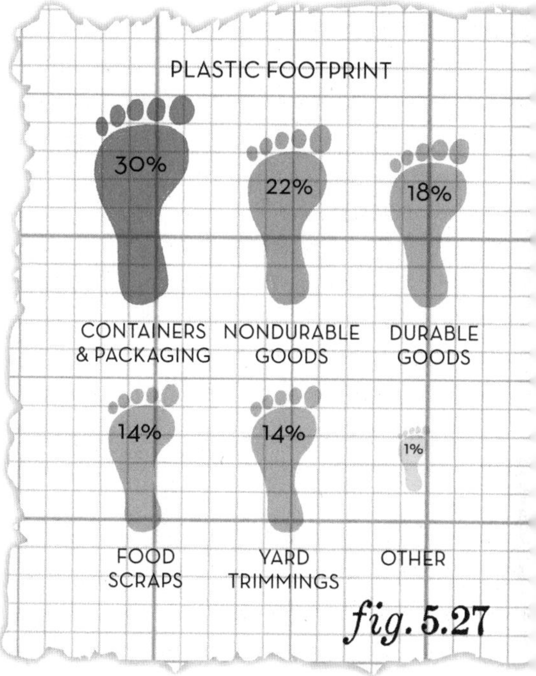

"No!"

"Yes. And every year, eight million more tons of plastic goes into the ocean."

PLASTIC FOOTPRINT

30% CONTAINERS & PACKAGING

22% NONDURABLE GOODS

18% DURABLE GOODS

14% FOOD SCRAPS

14% YARD TRIMMINGS

1% OTHER

fig. 5.27

"That is just stupid," says Watson, hiking up a ridge.

"As I have noted many times," adds Klink. "You humans are not the quickest learners."

Watson jumps over a small ravine.

"But how does all this footprint stuff and the Bio-Action Gizmo and the Gaia idea of Earth connect?"

Frank ducks under another broken tree branch. "'Connect' is exactly the right word. Everything is connected. Every action taken by every person on this planet has an effect."

Klank, listening, and trying to understand, looks suddenly uncomfortable. He stops. **"Watson, pull my finger."**

Watson, without thinking, pulls Klank's finger.

Klank releases a blurt of gas.

"Ohhhhhh peeeeyouuuu!" yells Watson.

"Thanks," says Klank. **"And—sorry."**

"We'll have to fix your methane tank when we get back home," says Frank.

The guys reach the top of the hill and look down. They see a white aluminum work-site trailer perched on the edge of a now huge ravine gouged out by the storm.

The trailer sports a familiar logo on its door.

"GRRRRRRRRRRRRRR." Klink, remembering the mining bucket that smashed him, actually growls.

"This is it," says Frank. "The guys responsible for messing up the preserve, messing up Klink and Klank, and messing up the planet."

"Should we knock?" asks Watson.

"Oh, I will knock," says Klink.

He charges the trailer at top speed while twirling his sledgehammers. He hits the door with a *BAAAAAM!* and smashes it wide open.

"Oh, I will help, too," says Klank.

He revs his chain saws to Screaming High and slashes an even bigger opening in the side of the trailer.

Frank and Watson jump inside.

"Stop right there!" shouts Frank.

"We know you are the ones wrecking the planet!" yells Watson.

Two figures, standing behind the desk, freeze, papers in hand.

But they are not exactly who Watson thought they were going to be.

Fred and Betty—the **EARTH/HEART** crew bosses—just as surprised as Watson, stop gathering their papers. They look up at what seems to be two very crazy kids and two very angry robots.

Watson yells again. "And we have just the invention to stop you!"

Fred and Betty don't say a word. They just stare.

But from behind Watson and Frank Einstein, a familiar, and annoying, voice asks, "Oh really?"

And another very familiar voice adds, "Ooooooh ooook."

25

YOU!" SAYS WATSON.

"You!" says T. Edison.

"Oooook!" says Mr. Chimp.

"What the heck is going on here?" says crew boss Betty.

"Nothing you need to know," says T. Edison. "You two are still fired. For messing up my profits! Now, get out of here!"

"Gladly," says crew boss Fred.

He and Betty grab the rest of their papers and hustle out of the trailer.

Frank and Watson and T. Edison and Mr. Chimp stand face-to-face . . . to face-to-face.

"You told us you had no connection with this operation messing up the preserve," says Watson. "But here you are. What *is* going on?"

T. Edison looks around. "I have no idea what you are talking about."

Frank Einstein walks over to the **EARTH/HEART** logo on the wall of the trailer. "You were right from the beginning, Watson." Frank peels away the **EARTH/HEART** sign, revealing the logo underneath.

"Oh, big deal," says T. Edison. "That doesn't mean anything."

"I knew it!" says Watson. "I knew you were the ones wrecking everything! And breaking Klink and Klank to pieces!"

"Yeah!" adds Klank, lifting his chain-saw arm.

"Yes." says Klink, raising his sledgehammer fist.

"And now Frank Einstein is going to wreck you and your planet-killing business with his new, amazing, simple invention—the **BIO-ACTION GIZMO**!" Watson brags.

"Ooooooh, I'm so scared," says T. Edison sarcastically.

But you can tell he is interested.

"So what does this new gizmo of yours do? Suck all the oil and gas out of the earth without hurting your precious planet?"

Frank holds the wrapped-up package in front of him.

"Much better than that. It has the power to save the planet. And it's another thing Watson was right about—it *is* incredibly simple."

Frank starts to unwrap the invention.

"And I am going to *give it to you.*"

Mr. Chimp grabs T. Edison and dives behind the metal desk for protection.

Klink and Klank roll up on either side of Frank.

Frank Einstein says, "I give you the human-species-saving, whole-Earth-changing, complete-all-connected-life-amazing . . ."

Watson, Klink, and Klank lean forward.

T. Edison and Mr. Chimp peek out from behind the safety of the desk.

Frank lifts his glorious invention triumphantly aloft.

"BIO . . . ACTION . . . GIZMO!"

Everyone stares.

There is a deafening silence.

"Oh my," says T. Edison. "Really? It looks like a bag. Made of rope."

"Ooook oook," adds Mr. Chimp.

"Precisely!" says Frank. "A do-it-yourself, recycled, multi-use, never-use-another-plastic-bag-again B.A.G."

Watson squints. "Wow. Not exactly what I was expecting…"

"And it's *simple*!" says Frank. "Simple to make. Nothing more than rope and knots. Simple to use. Simple to save Earth from fifteen hundred bits of plastic every person uses every year."

Klink makes some rapid calculations. "This is true," he

confirms. "Humans are using approximately one trillion plastic bags every year. And throwing all of them away. Polluting their own planet."

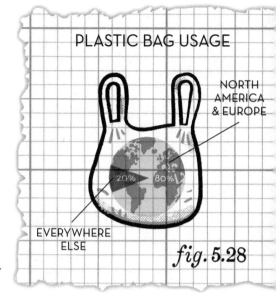

PLASTIC BAG USAGE

NORTH AMERICA & EUROPE

20% 80%

EVERYWHERE ELSE

fig. 5.28

"The **BIO-ACTION GIZMO** could drop that to nothing," figures Watson.

"And a trillion less plastic bits would be polluting Gaia."

T. Edison walks out from behind the desk.

Frank Einstein hands him the B.A.G. "And I am giving it to you."

T. Edison looks at the simple invention in his hands. He looks up at Frank and Watson. He looks over at Klink and Klank.

T. Edison thinks of snakes and ladders.

He speaks from his heart.

"You idiots."

T. Edison stomps his giant boot.

"Smart doesn't *win*. Being nice doesn't *win*. *Profits win!*"

T. Edison spots a potted plant that has fallen off a desk. He kicks the single red potted flower across the room.

"And you bumbling do-gooders are hurting my profits! I need to get rid of you doofnards once and for all."

Watson laughs. "Oh right. What are you going to do? Tie us up in this flimsy trailer and then leave and push it over into the ravine so it crashes down into the jagged rocks below and smashes me and Frank and Klink and Klank completely into bits and makes it look like we got caught in here during the storm that knocked the trailer over and no one ever knows you were behind it?"

"You know what?" says T. Edison. "That is a *great* idea."

He throws the **BIO-ACTION GIZMO** to Mr. Chimp.

"And use this to tie them up, Mr. Chimp. I think there is about to be a terrible storm-related Bio-Action accident."

Mr. Chimp grabs Watson and Frank.

"Klink and Klank . . . *attack!*" yells Watson.

Klink spins his hammers at top speed.

Klank revs his chain-saw hand.

From outside, you can hear wild smashing and crashing, and see the flimsy aluminum trailer rocking back and forth like you have never seen a trailer rock.

26

FRANK AND WATSON, KLINK AND KLANK SIT IN THE FOUR OFFICE chairs in the trailer, firmly tied with the rope from the Bio-Action Gizmo.

Klink stares at Watson.

"Hey, I didn't think he would really do it!"

Watson struggles against the rope. "And you guys were no help at all."

"Law One of the Three Laws of Robotics?" Frank reminds Watson. "A robot can not injure a human."

Watson scoots around in his chair. "Yeah, but it doesn't say anything about chimpanzees."

"You are both members of the hominid species," says Klink.

"Oooooooooo," fumes Watson. "Frank, you have to think up some genius plan to get us out of here. You always do. Come on!"

Frank Einstein tries to think up a genius plan.

Klink and Klank are disabled.

He and Watson are tied up.

None of them will survive a crash to the bottom of the ravine.

T. Edison and Mr. Chimp have just left the trailer.

The trailer begins to rock back and forth.

Frank Einstein thinks.

But no genius plan comes to mind.

"And hurry," says Watson. "This can't be the end of us!"

No plan at all comes to mind.

Klink calculates. "Actually, there is a very good possibility that this is the end of us."

"Noooooooooooo!" beeps Klank.

27

OOOHHHHH YES!" SAYS T. EDISON. "PUT SOME MUSCLE INTO IT. We've got profits to improve!"

Mr. Chimp re-grips the edge of the flimsy aluminum trailer, and rocks it up . . . down . . . higher up . . . down . . .

T. Edison sits on a nearby rock and reviews the **EARTH/HEART** drilling, mining, and logging numbers.

The trailer slides. It teeters over the edge of the ravine.

T. Edison talks to himself. "Drilling will take a day or two to get back up and running. Mining tomorrow. Logging on schedule . . . will finish off all the trees today . . ."

Mr. Chimp stops rocking the trailer.

Mr. Chimp stands over T. Edison.

"Ooooook?"

T. Edison squints up into Mr. Chimp's face and answers, "Yes, oooooook. We took down all the trees. Just this morning."

Mr. Chimp's brain hums.

He signs:

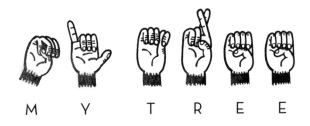

T. Edison flips over the **EARTH/HEART** lumber map.

"*Your* tree? Which one, the biggest tree? Of course." T. Edison checks his watch. "It's probably halfway to the lumberyard now. Huge profit!"

Mr. Chimp's vision goes narrow. His blood roars in his ears.

His brain hum goes from hum to high whine.

"So come on! Dump that trailer full of problems. And let's get going. Time is money, you know."

T. Edison gives Mr. Chimp a playful punch on the shoulder.

Which pushes Mr. Chimp completely over his personal edge.

Mr. Chimp takes a deep breath . . . leans his head back . . . and unleashes a truly primal scream. He rips off his vest and tie, tears them to shreds, and howls and pounds the ground, the trailer, the earth, the sky.

Mr. Chimp bares his teeth.

The trailer slips another bit.

T. Edison laughs a nervous laugh.

And then Mr. Chimp really and totally loses it—exploding into an all-out, unthinking, mad-feeling, pure animal rage.

28

DUSK IN THE MIDVILLE PRESERVE.

Earth, as always, spins on its axis, revolves around the sun.

The setting sun lights the western sky red, orange, gold.

A fisherman, walking along the bottom of the ravine, finds a white aluminum trailer crumpled and broken against the jagged boulders.

He looks inside, afraid of what he might see.

Windows, desks, files, chairs—all completely smashed.

A single red flower. Dead.

The fisherman looks around the rest of the trailer.

"Must have slid down in that big storm last night," the

fisherman mutters. "Good thing no one was in it when it went down."

But there is no explaining how the kid with the big boots and bad haircut got himself super-wedgied, spanked, and tied to a tree with all that knotted rope.

And he won't talk about it.

29

USK IN THE FAR-NORTHERN END OF THE MIDVILLE PRESERVE.

Earth, as always, spins on its axis, revolves around the sun.

The setting sun lights a nest of roughly woven branches high in a young oak tree.

In the nest, a dark-furred animal crouches over an invention.

Its long fingers pick and weave and twist and knot.

The animal finishes.

It holds its work up in the last light of the sun for inspection.

It is a bag.

A knotted rope bag.

A reusable, recycled, world-changing rope bag.

The animal looks over its shoulder at the first star of the evening just above the western horizon.

The animal thinks about the star, about its own star—the Sun, about the universe.

The animal decides . . .

"Oooook."

30

WATSON POKES A STICK IN THE FIRE THEY HAVE BUILT BEHIND Grampa Al's barn. A bright shower of orange sparks spirals up into the starry night.

"I never would have thought, in a million years, that we would ever be helped . . . not to mention saved . . . by T. Edison's chimp!"

Frank Einstein looks into the fire. "I don't think he is T. Edison's chimp anymore. If he ever was." Frank taps the fire-pit rocks with his own stick. "I wonder what happened? And what he might be up to?"

Klank hums, **"He might just want to be a chimpanzee."**

Klink adds, "Or the chimpanzee King of the World."

Frank leans back and looks up at all the stars spread across the inky blue sky. He spots the brightest light, low on the western horizon. The planet Venus. Sometimes called the evening star.

"Wooowwww. What a sight. It's got me thinking . . . ?"

Watson sits up. "No. We do not want to know what it's got you thinking. Because what you are thinking is probably just another way to get us almost killed! Again."

"What . . ." says Frank. "I was just thinking about our amazing planet. And how amazing other planets are. And that all the planets make our amazing solar system. And all those solar systems make galaxies. And all those galaxies–"

"That is true," confirms Klink. He pounds his hammer and reports, "This planet you call Earth is located in the Sol Solar System . . . of the Milky Way Galaxy . . . of the Local Group of Galaxies . . . of the Virgo Supercluster . . . of the Known Universe."

Frank points his stick toward their makeshift Wall of Science in the barn. "All making our final subject, our last column . . ."

Frank stirs the fire and sends up another wild spray of orange sparks. "Are you with me?"

"No," says Watson. "Absolutely not."

"Interesting," says Klink.

Klank looks uncomfortable. **"Watson, would you please pull my finger?"**

Watson, still worried about Frank's next idea, not thinking, pulls Klank's finger. And releases a loud *blatttt* of built-up gas.

Watson holds his nose. "Awwwwwwwww man!"

"Great!" says Frank Einstein. "I'll take that as three yeses."

Watson rolls around on the ground.

"Sorry," says Klank.

Frank laughs.

"OK, first we fix Klank. . . .

"And then we explore . . . the universe."

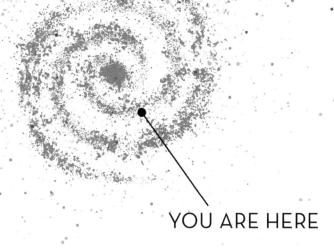

YOU ARE HERE

MATTER

ENERGY

HUMANS

Aristotle

$E=mc^2$

newton

Tesla

daVinci

LIFE

EARTH

UNIVERSE

Darwin

WATSON'S FAVORITE ACRONYMS
(AND INITIALISMS)

An ACRONYM is a word made by taking the initial letters (or groups of letters) in a series of words . . . and pronouncing them as a new word.

SCUBA	Self-Contained Underwater Breathing Apparatus
RADAR	RAdio Detection and Ranging
TASER	Adapted from the 1911 book by Victor Appleton, *Tom Swift and His Electric Rifle* Thomas A. Swift Electric Rifle
LASER	Light Amplification by Stimulated Emission of Radiation
SONAR	SOund NAvigation Radar
ZIP CODE	Zone Improvement Plan Code

An INITIALISM is like an acronym—you use the first letters of other words to make a word—but the difference is you pronounce each letter.

UFO	Unidentified Flying Object
SUV	Sport Utility Vehicle
FYI	For Your Information
MD	Medical Doctor
ADD	Attention Deficit Disorder
AKA	Also Known As
SOS	Save Our Souls
OK	(No one knows for sure . . .)

Here's a list of business acronyms and initialisms:

ADIDAS	Founder Adi (nickname for Adolph) Dassler
BVD	Bradley, Voorhees, and Day (originally women's undergarment makers)
CVS	Consumer Value Store
GEICO	Government Employees Insurance Company
M&MS	Forrest Mars and Bruce Murrie
NABISCO	National Biscuit Company
NECCO	New England Confectionery Company
SUNOCO	Sun Oil Company

GRAMPA AL'S
SHRINK YOUR
PLASTIC FOOTPRINT

Most of us don't know how much plastic we use and throw away. But we do know that it should be a lot less.

So here is what we can all do:
- Figure out how much plastic you use and throw away.
- Use less, and you throw away less.

STEP 1
- Get a notebook.
- Make a record of how much plastic you use and throw away in a day.
- Keep this record for a week.

STEP 2
- Look for ways you can use less plastic.
- Carry a reusable bag.
- Don't buy plastic individual water bottles.
- Don't use straws.

- Don't use plastic cups, utensils, or take-out containers.
- Recycle the plastic you do use.

- Follow the U.S. EPA (Environmental Protection Agency) slogan: *Reduce, Reuse, Recycle.*

- Look into online groups such as Plastic Bank, 5 Gyres, Ocean Conservancy, Life Without Plastic, Plastic-Free Tuesday, and Plastic Pollutes.

- Save the world.

FRANK EINSTEIN'S MAKE YOUR OWN
BIO-ACTION GIZMO

MATERIALS

1 hank of cotton clothesline

1 ball of string

KNOTS TO USE

Lark's Head Knot   Overhand Knot

1. Cut a section of clothesline about eight feet long. This
    is going to be the top of your bag and its two handles.

2. Cut sixteen sections of string, each four feet long.

3. Lay clothesline (rope) across a table. Weight or tie
    down ends.

4. Double each length of string.
    Start six inches in from one end of your rope.

Loop each of the sixteen doubled strings onto the rope with a Lark's Head Knot. Place them about one-and-a-half inches apart.

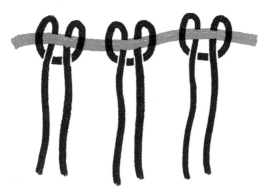

5. Beginning with the second and third string, tie an overhand knot about two-and-a-half inches down from the rope.

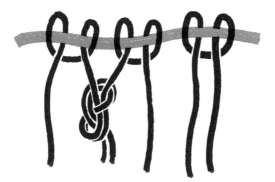

6. Tie the same overhand knot with the next two strings.
7. And the next two.

8. And the next two.

9. When you get to the last string, go back to the first two strings, go down another one-and-a-half inches, and tie another overhand knot.

10. Repeat, repeat, repeat . . . until you have a whole net hanging from your rope.

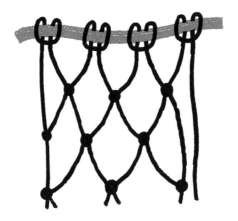

11. Tie an overhand knot in the end of your rope (this is to stop your next knot from slipping off the end).

12. Make the loop for the opening of your **B.A.G.** by forming a circle with the loose end of the rope. Tie it off with your Lark's Head Knot.

13. Complete the circle by tying the last untied string to the first string using overhand knots.

14. Make one handle by looping the rope back to the other side of the circle. Tie it there with another Lark's Head Knot.

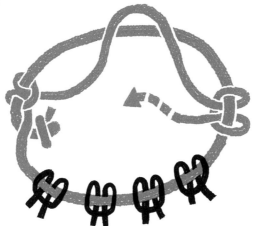

15. Make the second handle by tying the rope next to your first end knot. Using, guess what knot? That's right, the Lark's Head.

16. Tie off all of the hanging ends of the string together with any kind of knots you like in order to secure the bottom of your **B.A.G.**

17. Use your **BIO-ACTION GIZMO** wherever you go. Congratulate yourself for being part of the solution. Feel good about helping save our planet.

LUMPY THE LUMP OF COAL
"FOSSIL FUELS ARE COOL!" RAP

My name is Lumpy, the Lump of Coal,
And spreading the cool word about fossil fuels is my goal.

Coal, oil, and gas . . . are called fossil fuels,
Because they were made in the days before dinosaurs had duels.

We burn fossil fuels to make electricity and power,
For the lights and heat and cars and stuff we use every hour.

Once you use fossil fuels, they are no longer doable
Which is why this energy source is called "nonrenewable."

You might have heard noise about fossil fuels' greenhouse effect.
But just look around—our planet's not wrecked!

So if you want the cool power of millions of horses
Dig coal, oil, and gas—our dope fresh energy sources.

T. EDISON'S TOTALLY NOT-STOLEN
INVENTIONS FROM HIS NOTEBOOK

- **BUILD TWO ARTIFICIAL INTELLIGENCE ROBOTS.**

  Use parts around the shop.

  Wire electronic brains so they can teach themselves.

- **MAKE ANTI-MATTER COMBUSTION ENGINE.**

  Use energy created by combination
     of Matter and Antimatter.
  Use it as a motor for bike.

- **INVENT A PHONE THAT DOESN'T HAVE TO BE PLUGGED IN.**
  Maybe call it the *Edison Self Phone*.

- **DELIVERY SYSTEM FOR WIRELESS POWER.**
  Like lightning, static electricity from tip of finger . . .
  Call it the *Edison Electro-Hand*.

- **SOMETHING TO TURBO-BOOST BRAINWAVES.**

  Oh yes, something like a baseball cap.

  With a Brainwave Turbo.

  Call it the *Edison*

  BrainWaver.

- **A GLASS BULB THAT CAN PRODUCE LIGHT.**

  Make a tiny wire that can
    be heated with elec-
    tricity to glow.
  Surround it with a
    glass bulb.
  We should call it the
    Edison Light Bulb.

- **SOME KIND OF DEVICE TO SPEED UP EVOLUTION, FORWARD AND BACKWARD.**
  Crosswire a DNA splitter/rezipper into something like,
  oh, I don't know, a championship wrestling belt.
  Use it to hop around the evolutionary Circle of Life.
  Edison EvoBomber Belt would be a great name.

MR. CHIMP'S CHINESE
FINGER COUNTING

 1

 2

 3

 4

 5

 6

 7

 8

 9

 10

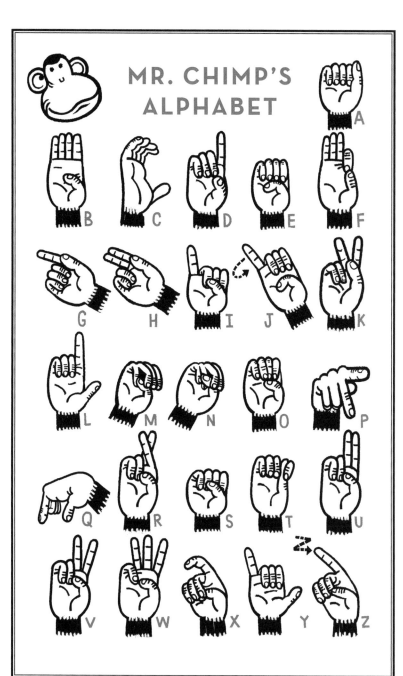

MR. CHIMP'S ALPHABET

JON SCIESZKA is a mammal living in the Holocene Epoch of the Cenozoic Era of the planet Earth. He is the author of a lot of books, the founder of Guys Read, and the first National Ambassador for Young People's Literature. He can usually be found near Latitude 40° 39′ 56″ N Longitude 73° 58′ 11″ W. And for the love of Gaia, he takes his Bio-Action Gizmo with him wherever he goes.

BRIAN BIGGS has illustrated enough books to fill thousands of plastic bags and circle the globe twenty-four times. He is the writer and illustrator of the Everything Goes series, as well as the Tinyville Town series for Abrams Appleseed. He lives in Philadelphia, Pennsylvania, where he worries about the climate as he sits on his porch watching the asphalt melt.

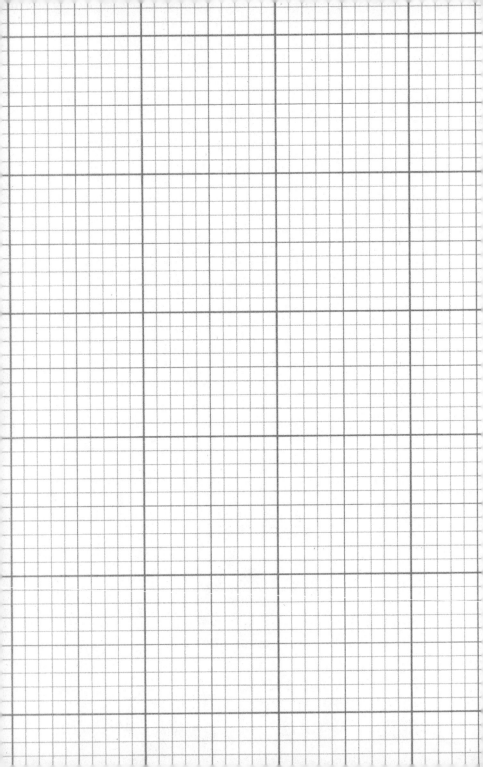

TO GAIA. FOR EVERYTHING.

PUBLISHER'S NOTE: THIS IS A WORK OF FICTION. NAMES, CHARACTERS, PLACES, AND INCI-
DENTS ARE EITHER THE PRODUCT OF THE AUTHOR'S IMAGINATION OR ARE FICTITIOUS, AND ANY
RESEMBLANCE TO ACTUAL PERSONS, LIVING OR DEAD, BUSINESS ESTABLISHMENTS, EVENTS,
OR LOCALES IS ENTIRELY COINCIDENTAL.

LIBRARY OF CONGRESS CATALOGING-IN-PUBLICATION DATA

NAMES: SCIESZKA, JON/BIGGS, BRIAN, AUTHOR. | SCIESZKA, JON. FRANK EINSTEIN; 5.

TITLE: FRANK EINSTEIN AND THE BIO-ACTION GIZMO / BY JON SCIESZKA AND BRIAN BIGGS.

DESCRIPTION: NEW YORK: AMULET BOOKS, AN IMPRINT OF ABRAMS, 2017. | SERIES: FRANK
EINSTEIN; 5 | SUMMARY: BOY GENIUS AND INVENTOR FRANK EINSTEIN AND HIS ROBOT PALS
KLINK (INTELLIGENT) AND KLANK (SORT-OF INTELLIGENT) STUDY THE SCIENCE OF ECOLOGY
AND CONSERVATION AS THEY TRY TO STOP CLASSMATE AND ARCHRIVAL T. EDISON AND HIS
LOGGERS FROM DESTROYING THE MIDVILLE FOREST PRESERVE.

IDENTIFIERS: LCCN 2016044182 | ISBN 978-1-4197-2297-4

SUBJECTS: LCSH: INVENTORS—JUVENILE FICTION. | ROBOTS—JUVENILE FICTION.
| ECOLOGY—JUVENILE FICTION. | NATURE CONSERVATION—JUVENILE FICTION. | CYAC:
INVENTORS—FICTION. | ROBOTS—FICTION. | ECOLOGY—FICTION. | CONSERVATION OF
NATURAL RESOURCES—FICTION. | SCIENCE FICTION. | HUMOROUS STORIES. | LCGFT:
SCIENCE FICTION. | HUMOROUS FICTION.

CLASSIFICATION: LCC PZ7.S4I267 FRH 2017 | DDC 813.54 [FIC]—DC23

LC RECORD AVAILABLE AT HTTPS://LCCN.LOC.GOV/2016044182

PAPERBACK ISBN 978-1-4197-3125-9

TEXT COPYRIGHT © 2017, 2018 JRS WORLDWIDE LLC
ILLUSTRATIONS COPYRIGHT © 2017, 2018 BRIAN BIGGS
BOOK DESIGN BY CHAD W. BECKERMAN

AMULET BOOKS ARE AVAILABLE AT SPECIAL DISCOUNTS WHEN PURCHASED IN QUANTITY
FOR PREMIUMS AND PROMOTIONS AS WELL AS FUNDRAISING OR EDUCATIONAL USE.
SPECIAL EDITIONS CAN ALSO BE CREATED TO SPECIFICATION. FOR DETAILS, CONTACT
SPECIALSALES@ABRAMSBOOKS.COM OR THE ADDRESS BELOW.

AMULET BOOKS® IS A REGISTERED TRADEMARK OF HARRY N. ABRAMS, INC.

ABRAMS The Art of Books
195 Broadway, New York, NY 10007
abramsbooks.com

"HUGE LAUGHS AND GREAT SCIENCE."
—MAC BARNETT, *THE TERRIBLE TWO*

6

FRANK EINSTEIN

and the
SPACE-TIME
ZIPPER

C

B

A

THE *NEW YORK TIMES* BESTSELLING SERIES

JON SCIESZKA ILLUSTRATED BY BRIAN BIGGS

FRANK EINSTEIN

and the SPACE-TIME ZIPPER

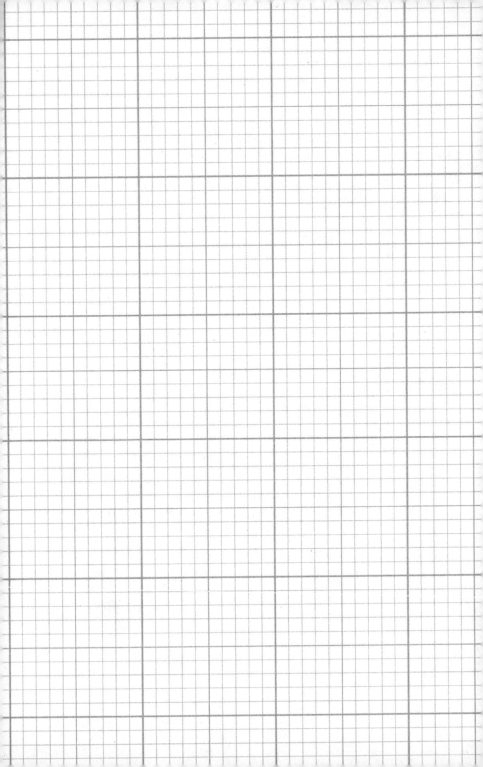

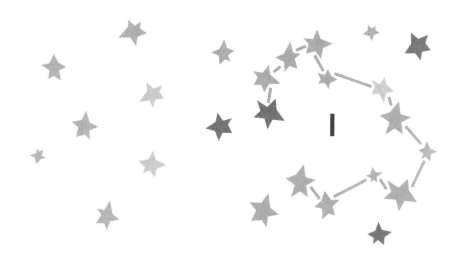

THE SUN SETS SLOWLY IN THE WESTERN SKY OF MIDVILLE.

Watson zips down East Oak Street as fast as he can pedal.

From the other side of town, Janegoodall races along West Oak Street.

They both hit the corner of Oak and Pine at almost exactly the same moment, skid, slide, turn, and stop.

Watson holds up his phone. "You got the weird text from Frank, too?"

Janegoodall nods. "What do you think it means?"

Watson shakes his head. "I have no idea what's going on . . . but it sounds like Frank's in trouble."

Janegoodall reads from her phone. "Need help. Come to junkyard. Follow the arrow sign. At sunset. Bring banana."

Watson holds up a slightly smushed banana.

Janegoodall shakes her head. "I have no idea."

Watson looks at the setting sun. "Let's roll!"

Watson and Janegoodall race their bikes to Grampa Al Einstein's house/Fix It! repair shop and Frank Einstein's laboratory.

They skid to a stop, drop their bikes, race around the back of Grampa Al's.

They scan the piles of junk.

"There," says Watson.

Janegoodall and Watson follow the old lightbulb-studded arrow sign.

But it points to nothing except a pile of broken toasters.

The red-orange rays of the setting sun light the top of the giant maple tree in the alley.

Watson jams the banana in his back pocket. "Frank needs help with . . . toasters?"

Janegoodall looks around. "Maybe this is the wrong sign." She kicks at a pile of junk. She sees metal.

Janegoodall and Watson clear away the toasters. But the metal turns out to be nothing but a storm drain.

A crow caws in the distance.

Venus, the evening star, glows silver in the gathering dusk.

"Are we too late?"

"Maybe we missed sunset."

Janegoodall and Watson look up.

And that's when they hear a metallic clink. A knocking on the storm sewer cover.

Watson and Janegoodall kneel down, use two rusted metal rods to pry up the metal disk.

"Frank . . . ?"

2

SPACE.

Outer space.

Hundreds . . . no, thousands . . . no, millions of points of light dot the moonless inky blue-black night sky.

A kid wearing size-five brown wing-tip shoes swings a giant telescope in a slow arc. He scans the points of starlight.

"Wow!"

Standing next to the kid, a chimpanzee in a lab coat, pleasantly surprised for once, agrees.

The sparkly expanse of the Milky Way, splashed across the sky, is . . . wow.

"Look at all of those stars. All of those suns. So many planets."

Mr. Chimp nods.

"If we could find a way to travel out there . . . just think . . . we could . . ."

Mr. Chimp nods again, his mind expanding with thoughts of the sheer immensity of the universe. The sheer immensity of *possibilities*. He is glad he came back. Glad T. Edison might be of some help in his Big Plan.

". . . make so . . . much . . . money!"

Mr. Chimp covers his face with his hands.

If it weren't so dark in the rooftop observatory of Chimp-Edison Laboratories, you could see him shaking his head. Now less glad.

T. Edison shuts down his telescope. He closes up the observatory. He flicks on the lights.

"But other planets, other solar systems, are so far away."

T. Edison paces back and forth. He looks over his planet charts.

"It takes too many years to get anywhere."

Mr. Chimp slides his hands down his face. This is the first smart thing he has heard T. Edison say tonight.

Mr. Chimp signs:

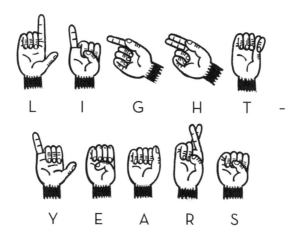

L I G H T -

Y E A R S

"Exactly!" says T. Edison. "The distance that light can travel, speeding nearly 300,000 kilometers per second." T. Edison starts pacing again. "I'll bet you didn't know that!"

Mr. Chimp sits down and writes out the mathematical formula for the distance of one light-year.

Mr. Chimp holds up his calculation.

This annoys T. Edison.

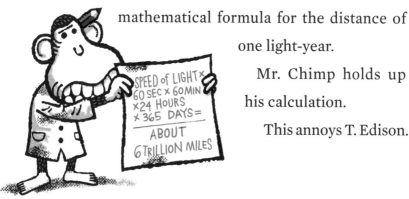

SPEED of LIGHT ×
60 SEC × 60 MIN
× 24 HOURS
× 365 DAYS =
————————
ABOUT
6 TRILLION MILES

"Well, maybe you did know. But here is my genius idea—what if I invent a way to travel *faster* than light? Then we could get to any planet. In seconds. Like taking a train. A very fast train."

Mr. Chimp looks up from his calculations. He doesn't even know where to start.

He could remind T. Edison that nothing can outrace light.

He could explain to T. Edison that when a car traveling at the speed of light turns on its lights . . . the light still travels at the speed of light.

He could explain to T. Edison the vast scale of the universe.

That if Earth were the size of a tennis ball, the sun would be seven football fields away. The next closest star would be 130,000 miles away. The next galaxy unimaginably far away.

But Mr. Chimp is tired of explaining things to T. Edison.

Plus—this time, he's got a plan of his own.

Mr. Chimp gathers up his papers, looks at T. Edison, and lies:

G R E A T

I D E A

Mr. Chimp waves good-night.

And heads off to his own room.

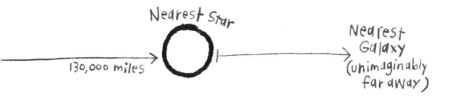

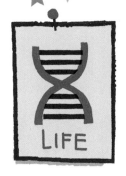
LIFE

EARTH

UNIVERSE

ALSO AVAILABLE:

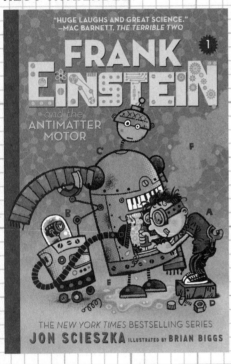

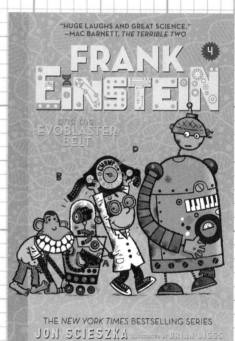

TO FIND OUT WHAT HAPPENS NEXT, READ
FRANK EINSTEIN AND THE SPACE-TIME ZIPPER